Lilly Sommers was [illegible] much of her childhood [illegible] New South Wales. The past is one of her maj[or interests and she probably] began writing about it because it was the next best thing to being there. Her other interests include gardening and reading. She currently lives in Bendigo, Victoria, with her husband and two children.

LILLY SOMMERS

WHEN SHADOWS FALL

ARROW

An Arrow book
published by
Random House Australia Pty Ltd
20 Alfred Street, Milsons Point, NSW 2061
http://www.randomhouse.com.au

Sydney New York Toronto
London Auckland Johannesburg
and agencies throughout the world

First published 1998
Copyright © Lilly Sommers 1998

National Library of Australia
Cataloguing-in-Publication Data

Sommers, Lilly.
When shadows fall.

ISBN 0 09 183514 3.

   I. Title.

A823.3

Typeset by Asset Typesetting Pty Ltd, Sydney
Printed by Griffin Press, Adelaide

10 9 8 7 6 5 4 3 2

To all who made this book possible

1

The rough weather conditions over Bass Strait rattled the aircraft and several times it dropped, taking my stomach with it. I glanced about at the pale, tense faces of the other passengers, wondering if they were reviewing their lives, and finding them wanting. In a way I was invincible. I had brushed death so close, it did not frighten me any more. When we landed at Hobart airport, the storm rumbled overhead, spitting lightning and pouring rain, and then dispersed as if it had never been.

The sun shone.

I collected my luggage and went over to the hire car counter, and then had to wait for my request to be processed. The chair was hard and unfriendly, and I watched the passing human stream with indifferent eyes, their impatience, excitement and, occasionally, sorrow not touching me at all. It was as though I were watching the world through bars, locked away on my own. And that was exactly how I had felt these past six months. The passionate woman who had channelled everything into her life and work now seemed like someone else.

'Wouldn't you rather have other people around you?' Bolten had asked me, his sharp eyes compassionate.

I had hesitated, wondering how I could explain it to him. I had many friends, and at first they had rallied around me. But as time went on, I found I preferred my own company. Especially when the headaches started. I thought now of the past five years and the hectic pace I had set for myself. Never a moment alone, always the push and drive and ambition that had in the end made me famous. My life had been shaped and moulded, sometimes by forces beyond my control. And Ian had been there, from the first day. My husband and manager, my lover and friend.

He and I had been going to a party the night it happened. Driving through the rainy streets of Melbourne. Strangely, we'd been having one of our very rare arguments. I don't know how it had started, but one word had led to another, and suddenly the thing had flared up into a full-scale war.

He said things that hurt, and so did I. I knew we would have apologised and made up later. I knew it ... I clung to it. But we never had a chance. All in an instant, the other car had come at me from a side street, I tried to turn to avoid it, skidded on the wet road, and hit a tree.

Ian died that night. I had been only slightly injured, not even badly enough to stop me working. I had finished the film. But the headaches had begun not long afterwards, excruciating things that no amount of over-the-counter cures could dull. I'd had X-rays and brain scans and other tests I'd never heard of. They'd examined my skull inside and out, and found nothing. The headaches went on.

But it was more than that.

The headaches seemed to be a catalyst, and the disintegration of my life followed. I was due to begin another movie a month later, but my ability to put myself fully into a new role had deserted me. I was floundering, directionless. As if Ian had been the pivot around which I turned, and now he was dead, I could no longer function. The movie would begin with or without me, I knew that. Memories can be very short in show business, and all actors are expendable. There was always someone newer, better and younger looming on the horizon. I needed to get my act together again, before it was too late.

That was what this journey was all about.

Finding myself—I winced at the cliché—and Tasmania was just the place to find oneself. Tall mountains and misty rain, cold lakes and lonely fishermen, pretty cottages and green hills. So many corners where one could be alone.

'I'm always here,' Bolten had said. 'If you feel at all concerned, call me.' There was a genuineness in his voice.

I had smiled the smile Ian had loved. Wide and confident, it had once beamed out from countless glossy magazines, here and overseas. Only now the confidence wavered about the edges, as if another, more sensitive self had taken my place. And the eyes which had gazed so straight and sure were shadowed by pain and unhappiness … and guilt. Ian was dead and I was alive. And it was as if his death had released a new Kate O'Hara, a stranger in familiar clothing.

'Miss O'Hara?'

I looked up sharply. The girl had obviously been calling my name for some time—her smile had grown rigid.

'We have your car, Ms O'Hara. If you'll just sign these papers?' She lifted her voice brightly at the end of the sentence.

I signed the papers, barely glancing at them.

'Excuse me, Ms O'Hara,' and the girl's voice had lost its professional brittleness. 'Weren't you in *The Lost Ones?*'

She was wearing that half-scared, half-fascinated expression that said 'celebrity'. I was used to that look, and I smiled. 'Yes, I was.' The film had done better than anyone had expected at the box office and picked up a number of awards along the way. I had been pleased with my performance, surprised that the poised woman on the screen was me, two weeks after losing Ian.

'Are you staying long?' the girl was asking, looking suddenly very young.

I focused my thoughts. 'Three weeks. I'm leasing a cottage.' A cottage far from the late nights, early mornings and half-hysteria that characterised many movie-making ventures. A cottage far from Bolten's tests and the bright lights of hospitals, and places that reminded me of Ian and set the memories humming in my head. A cottage where I would take myself and my life in hand and decide what to do with both.

'Oh …' The girl was looking disappointed. 'I thought you might be making a film here.'

'Not this time.' And I smiled goodbye, collected up my luggage and walked towards the automatic doors.

I found the car, a late model. I took a moment to examine the dashboard and familiarise myself with the various dials and knobs and switches before starting the engine. The car park was nearly empty, and I had no trouble turning out onto the street and following the signs.

I was used to driving in the city, used to the aggressive tug and pull of drivers trying to be first to the lights and first to get away, and I had automatically geared myself up for such a battle. But now, as the kilometres slipped by, the tension drained out of me. I gazed about at the green hills and gentle hollows, and felt a kind of unfamiliar peace stealing into my soul.

Then I saw the river.

The real estate agent I had dealt with in Melbourne, Robert Tuck—'Call me Bob'—had been familiar with Tasmania. 'I left when I was eighteen,' he said, with a wistful look. 'Life moves at a slower pace down there.'

'It sounds ideal,' I smiled.

'Leeward is one of those pretty postcard sort of places,' he went on, smiling back. 'A bit of a tourist trap, I'm afraid, but unspoiled for all that. It's about ten minutes' drive north from Leeward to get to the cottage. It's been in my family for over a hundred years, but as far as I know we've never lived in it permanently. A holiday cottage.'

'The cottage by the river.'

'That's right.' He picked up his pen, turning it from end to end nervously. 'I did explain to you, didn't I, Ms O'Hara? The cottage is a bit, well, primitive.'

'No mod cons?' I murmured, making a joke of it.

He smiled, but still looked concerned. 'It *is* connected to the electricity, but that's so unreliable it hardly counts. And there are no near neighbours. You'll be quite cut off from the outside world.'

'It sounds … isolated,' I agreed.

'Exactly!' Bob seemed to think that as an actress, I would find such circumstances insupportable. Wither from lack of attention, perhaps. Ian would have hated it. The thought surfaced, mocking me. I shut it away.

I leaned forward towards Bob. 'Look, that doesn't matter to me. You see, I want to do some painting. It used to be a hobby of mine and I've hardly touched a brush for years. I want my own company for a couple of weeks. Don't worry, I'll be all right.'

But I had seen the doubt lingering in his eyes.

I followed the river, more or less. The waters would flash silver through the trees, and then vanish for a time as the road veered away. But always, the two pursued the same destiny, as if they had no choice. I wondered whether it really mattered that I had trained as an actor and become famous. Did anything that anyone did really matter? There was only ever one end to the story, wasn't there? No matter how many corners turned and how many detours taken, the destination was the same for everyone. Eventually. Some, like Ian, just got there sooner than others.

'Grim thoughts, Kate,' I murmured to myself, and turned on the radio. The music suited the scenery and I let it soothe me like the swirl of a paint brush, blending and softening my emotions. It had been a long time since I had painted. I didn't even know if I still could paint. Like so many things, I had put it on hold while I built my career. *Focus, Kate,* Ian used to say. *Focus on what's important.* And that meant my acting career.

After a while, I stopped for take-away coffee and a sandwich and a few supplies for the cottage. The air was sweet and clear and I breathed it in with pleasure. When I started off again, the river was back beside me, and now I felt its presence like an old friend.

I knew a little of Tasmania's history, some remembered from my schooldays and some picked up from novels and television and movies. I knew that it had been called Van Diemen's Land in the old days, and had been a penal settlement, a place of punishment. Macquarie Harbour, a lonely, savage place on the west coast, had been called Hell's Gates by those unfortunate enough to be sent there. Port Arthur, a top tourist destination, still retained a sense of suffering, overlaid now by the tragedy of the more recent dead.

As I drove, more of Tasmania's past came back to me. Bushrangers such as Brady and Cash and Howe had terrorised the early settlers, and the Tasmanian Aborigines had been almost wiped out. Tasmania's roads had been famous when those in the rest of the country were nothing but dirt tracks. Road gangs swung picks and shovelled and carted stone to build them. The bridges in Tasmania were some of the oldest in

Australia. And now—I looked about at the soft, wistful landscape—one would never know that this beautiful place harboured such a dark and grim past.

Eventually, the road sign to Leeward came up, and I realised the little town was just ahead. The sign told me that Leeward was 'A Tidy Town' as well as a 'Historic Town'. Good for Leeward, I thought.

My car topped a rise and there, clustered in a hollow in the hills, was a pleasant jumble of wooden and stone buildings, softened by huge old English trees. It was early autumn and the leaves were just turning to golds and reddy-oranges. They glowed like precious jewels by the riverside and in the streets of the little town.

I slowed down to the regulation speed limit. Leeward, from what I could see of it, consisted of a couple of shops, a garage and a pub. The place had the sort of smug confidence that historic towns gain over years of being told how pretty they are.

Leeward dozed in the late afternoon sun, watching me pass with half-closed, incurious eyes. And then it was fading in my rear-view mirror, and the bush enclosed me. The river sparkled a moment beside the road and then was gone, hidden behind trees and the slope of a hill. Sunlight flickered through the leaves and branches, making my eyes ache. I wondered, uneasily, if it would bring on one of the blinding headaches which had first sent me to see Bolten.

Not much further, I told myself.

There was the turn off, just where Bob Tuck had said it would be. A strip of bitumen through two rough fence posts and what remained of a gate, dragged to one side and left to rot. I slowed down carefully and turned in.

The hire car bounced and rattled over the potholes—the road would be a nightmare to negotiate after rain. Halfway along, the gravel suddenly gave way to dirt road. The car jolted and stalled. I restarted it grimly, going forward at a laboured crawl.

The trees were thicker here, and I felt as if I were heading deeper into the bush rather than towards a holiday cottage. The light seemed dimmer, the air chillier. I wondered suddenly, uneasily, if I were on the right road after all.

I had just decided to stop and turn back when the road widened out into a turning circle and there, before me, was the back of the cottage. And beyond it, the shimmering silver waters of the river.

I stopped the car and sat, just staring.

The cottage was built of grey blocks of stone, probably hand cut. Compared to the mellow, ethereal buildings in Leeward, it seemed solid and uncompromising. Here I am, it said, take me or leave me.

There were vines growing over part of the back wall—a futile attempt to soften that intractable look. Tendrils reached out to begin to encircle a water tank nearby. Bob had warned me the cottage did not have town water.

The garden was overgrown, clumps of scented geraniums and kiss-me-quick amongst sprawling white daisies and purple veronicas, and the bush crowding in. It had a wonderful feel to it; one would never know what might be under the leaves, waiting to be found.

Is this where I 'find myself', I wondered, in this silent, abandoned place?

After the hum of the car and the jarring rattle of the potholes, the quiet was like a solid thing, encasing me and the cottage. The idea made me shiver, and then I laughed at my own thoughts. It was just that I was used to the rush of the city—even the song of a bird in my tiny backyard was played to an accompaniment of passing traffic, lawn mowers and neighbours' quarrels.

I opened the car door and climbed out.

Now I could see that there was a narrow, roughly paved path leading around the side of the cottage. I negotiated abundant shrubs and slippery, moss-covered bricks, and found myself on an open verandah at the front of the cottage. Before me, the ground fell away, gently at first and then more steeply, towards a tiny jetty.

And the river.

Spellbound, I looked across the stretch of water. How far was it to the other side? I had never been good at judging distances. The land over there was a patchwork of greens and browns and soft blues. A tractor droned in the far distance, and cows groaned, impatient to be milked.

A bird flew low over the water, almost touching the surface. As I watched it landed neatly, settling its wings, and floated.

Behind me a cricket began to rasp, gathering strength from the fading light. The sun was slanting across the top of the cottage, throwing long shadows down the grassy bank. I took a deep breath, and felt as if I were breathing in something wonderful. Another deep breath and I turned from my inspection of the river, back to the cottage.

The verandah was narrow, only about three paces wide, and the bricks that paved it had been worn down by the years into a series of shallow peaks and troughs. A couple of old milk churns did service as pots for plants—tough-looking scarlet geraniums. Either side of the door was a little window, the glass freshly cleaned. Bob had told me that one of the locals kept an eye on the place and, before my arrival, would arrange for a thorough cleaning.

The cleaning had not extended to the outside, I thought with amusement. Someone's old gumboots waited loyally beside the door, and a bird had made a nest under a corner of the eaves, speckling the verandah with a pattern of white and black droppings.

On the other side of the cottage, the bush had closed in on an old gum tree. Twisted and torn by the years, it bowed precariously over the roof. The setting sun shone through the leaves, reddening them to the colour of blood. The shadows dripped.

Bob had warned me that it was primitive. Certainly not everyone's idea of a holiday house. But then I was not on an ordinary holiday. A feeling of calm contentment welled up inside me. Almost as if I belonged here. The feeling was so unfamiliar and so intense, it was a moment before I could bring myself out of it.

It's getting dark, Kate, I thought, amused. Are you going to stand out here all night, communing with nature, or are you going to take a look inside?

I searched in my purse for the key. There was a new lock in the door, all shiny and reassuring. I wondered, surprised, whether they had much trouble with thieves here. Housebreaking seemed so much a city problem, and Leeward was surely too small and too isolated to be the sort of place chosen by lawless refugees from the city.

I creaked open the mesh door, and slid the key into the heavy old wooden door. The lock turned silently and the door swung in. The darkness came to meet me, heavy with the musty odour of neglect and the sharper, newer smell of pine disinfectant.

I climbed the single step, and found that I was standing in a narrow passageway which ran from the front to the back of the cottage. It really wasn't as dark as I had first thought. It was just that the sun was now behind the cottage; in the morning it would be beaming through those front windows, filling the place with light.

A door to my left led to a small, gloomy room with a covered window. I went in and leaned across a sofa to haul up the moth-eaten Roman blind. Now I could see that this was a sitting room. It was furnished with old bits and pieces, nothing matching.

'Decor by St Vincent de Paul,' I murmured, looking around. There was a lumpy sofa and two threadbare armchairs, as well as a coffee table which looked as if it had been hammered together in a woodwork class by somebody's son. The bookcase was constructed of planks and bricks, and the cupboard was seriously water-damaged. There was an open fireplace, hidden behind a faded arrangement of dried flowers, with a pile of neatly stacked logs in a basket on a corner of the hearth. A painting hung above the mantel, very dark and Victorian-looking.

The bedroom was on the opposite side of the cottage. A double bed had been squeezed into the little room, the flowered quilt freshly laundered. A narrow wardrobe held a few bits and pieces belonging to previous occupants, including a hat and thongs. A carved box wafted camphor when I lifted the lid, and contained spare sheets and blankets.

There was a tiny bathroom-cum-laundry at the back of the cottage, with a stone trough and something that looked suspiciously like a rusty flat iron. I picked it up curiously, feeling the weight of it. Imagine, I thought, being a woman a hundred years ago. I almost felt the heat of the fire, heard the constant thump of the iron, smelt the clean, crisp linen.

The image hovered at the edges of my mind, a shadow against the light, and then dissolved and was gone. I put the iron back gently, and went to explore the kitchen.

It was also small, but had everything I would need for my stay. A wood-burning stove that looked as if it had done good service, a small fridge which did not appear to be working at the moment, a sink and cupboard and a table. There was a good supply of crockery and cutlery, oddments and remnants, nothing matching. A large lamp had been placed on the table, and beside it a couple of candles, a tarnished candle holder, and a box of matches with the name of a motel chain printed across the cover.

After a brief search, I found the overhead light switch on the wall, and flicked it. As I feared, nothing. I tried again, but it made no difference. Bob had told me the electricity supply was dodgy. 'I'll just have to pretend I'm Florence Nightingale,' I joked to myself. After Bob's warning, I had gone out and bought myself a good torch and plenty of batteries, as well as a portable cassette player.

'I'll soon get used to doing without,' I told myself firmly. 'Pretend it's a film set. *Wuthering Heights*!'

But the words fell flat. Ian's face came into my mind, so solid and real he could have been standing before me. *What the hell are you doing here?* he asked me, eyes glinting with the half-smile he knew always won me over. *Focus, Kate, for God's sake!*

Three weeks, I thought nervously. Could I really survive three weeks here, all alone? Did I want to?

'Leeward's only just up the road,' I said aloud. 'And the cottage is very ... cosy.'

And, Ian said in my head, *you can always pack up and go home. Back to the real world.*

'Yes,' I sighed. 'There's that.' I went to fetch my luggage. Outside, the day was settling down to evening. Soon it would be too dark to see. Back inside the cottage again, I opened all the windows and pulled up the blinds, and then I went into the kitchen and inspected the lamp.

How difficult can this be? I asked myself. The bowl of the lamp was transparent, and I could see the fuel inside. Plenty of it. There was a knob on the side of the bowl, no doubt for increasing the flow of fuel to the wick. The glass lifted off easily, and I saw that the wick was black with use. Well then, it must work! And when I turned the knob and struck a match, the wick did catch well enough. The acrid scent made my nose twitch and, carefully, I set the glass cover back over the flame. I watched it flicker, brighten for a moment ... and die.

Slowly, patiently, I went through the process again. And again the light died. The third time, my hands were shaking. I felt tears sting my eyes and was powerless to stop them. This time the match broke and I let it fall. Slowly I sat down on one of the sturdy old chairs, put my elbows on the table and my head in my hands. The tears slid down my chin and wet my sleeves.

Suddenly I was back in my worst nightmare. The grey night, the blur of car lights, the rain against the windscreen, almost too heavy for the wipers to cope. And Ian's voice, shouting, his face twisted in anger. 'I'm always there for you!' he was saying. 'What the hell have you got to complain about?'

'You ask that!' I screamed. 'How can you ask that?'

'You're selfish, Kate! You always have been!'

And then we had hit the tree, and there was only silence.

The headaches had started after I had finished shooting the movie. Bolten performed numerous examinations and then one day he called me into his office for a chat. 'There's another possibility, you know,' he said. 'These headaches may not have a physical cause at all.'

Until then, I hadn't even considered such an explanation of my problem. I stared at him blankly. Bolten smiled reassuringly. 'It's just a possibility, Ms O'Hara. Headaches can stem from what we call "stress" or grief or guilt. Do you see what I'm getting at?'

Psychosomatic! He thinks you feel guilty because I died and you're alive, Ian's amused voice informed me. *He thinks you feel like you killed me. Did you kill me, Kate?* Suddenly I felt cold and afraid. What would Bolten say if I told him Ian spoke to me in my head?

'I don't believe I could imagine such pain,' I had replied in a voice that trembled. 'I don't believe it.'

Bolten nodded, watching me. 'Well,' he said. 'In that case, we'll do some more tests. I'll arrange for you to spend a few days in hospital.' He went on, listing various medical procedures. He sounded professional, clever and kind. But I had stopped listening to him. Suddenly I was so tired I could hardly keep my eyes open. And I knew I couldn't face any more tests, not yet. I needed some time alone, that's what it was. How long was it since I had had a holiday? Not a weekend away, promoting myself and mingling, but a proper old-fashioned holiday? It was so long, I couldn't even remember.

When I blurted the words out, Bolten lifted his eyebrows. And later, when I told him where I was going, he hadn't liked the idea of my being on my own at the cottage. But I had insisted. What could he do? Forbid it? No, I wanted time and space to come to terms with my life and myself. My career was at a crisis point, and now Bolten was suggesting my headaches were psychosomatic. The frightening thing was, perhaps he was right.

The past gave way to the present. I was sitting in the dark, crying as I hadn't cried for a long time.

I drew a shaky breath and wiped my face with my palms, sniffing loudly.

'Pull yourself together, Kate O'Hara!' I said to myself. I did, just. But I felt as if I were bound together with a very cheap brand of sticky tape, likely to come apart again at any moment.

Picking up the matches once more, I stuck a candle into the candle holder and lit it. The flame wavered ineffectually, then brightened. Soon I would try to light the stove and boil the kettle. But not just yet.

I walked to the door and peered out through the mesh—both doors and windows were mesh-covered to keep out the insects. Outside, the evening light had gone, the last gleam on the water had faded. I stared into the darkness, listening.

Crickets sang, and a frog croaked inter-mittently, lazily, as if it had all the time in the world. Somewhere far away, a car roared and faded. The stars began to twinkle in the velvet of the sky and a big moon slowly rose. A faint breeze stirred the old gum tree beside the cottage, causing its leaves to brush on the roof and some of the branches to tap like fingers knocking against the primitive guttering.

For a moment, I thought I saw a movement in the darkness, a shape on the river. But then it was gone, blending into the shadows. I shivered, suddenly cold, and closed the door on the night, locking myself in with my thoughts.

2

I slept heavily and woke late. Sunlight was already pouring in through the windows, and the birds were full of noisy contentment. I realised I had forgotten to close the windows last night, despite my caution in locking the front door.

I lay a moment, preparing myself to rise and begin the day. It was odd, but I had had no trouble sleeping since Ian died. It was the waking hours I had difficulty with. Sleep was easy, a relief, in a way. If I could, I would have spent all day and night sleeping. Sleep meant I didn't have to think.

The kettle was cold, and I shoved a new piece of wood into the stove as well as some kindling. It had taken me several tries last night, but I had finally got the fire to burn without billowing smoke. Burn enough, at least, to boil the kettle. I hadn't attempted to cook any food, but had made do with a few sandwiches left over from the drive down. Hardly designed to 'build up my strength'. I had always been slim—well, let's be honest, thin. I couldn't afford not to eat. And yet lately I had found it difficult to keep up the pretence of a good appetite.

There didn't seem much point.

The kettle began to steam, and I made my cup of tea and took it outside onto the verandah. The sun slanted in, warming my bare feet, and I sipped the hot, strong brew, watching the river.

The light was fascinating. It glittered in waves across the surface, blinding me, like molten gold and silver. From time to time a breeze would ripple the surface and the light would break into a million pieces, scattering like diamonds.

This would be a challenge to paint!

'But first I must get some supplies in,' I told myself aloud. And listened to my voice, husky with disuse, float out across the water.

Leeward was as quiet as it had been the day before, warming slowly to the sun. I supposed most of the residents either worked in a larger town, or owned one of the 'tourist traps' Bob Tuck had told me about.

As well as the general store, the pub and the garage, there were a number of houses whose front rooms had been turned into showplaces for antiques or crafts; one of them was now a small café and bakery.

A plaque in the main street stated in bold black writing that Leeward had been established in 1810 by settlers looking for land. The road had been built by convicts, who had a barracks to the north of the town. A fire in 1829 razed this to the ground and there was a mass escape, but all had been recaptured without incident.

So much for Leeward, I thought.

I collected my groceries and carried the bags back to the car. Although friendly enough, no-one seemed to recognise me or was even particularly interested in me, and I was glad of that. I didn't want curious questions. I had not come here to promote my movies. I had come to be just plain Kate O'Hara, amateur artist.

The road was as rough and potholed as I remembered and I bumped my way towards the river. On reaching the cottage, I pulled up and sat a moment in the car, as I had done yesterday. It really was a peaceful place. A couple of bright parrots flitted in the trees, and a long-legged water bird glided with kitelike wings across the river, circling for a landing. Bees hummed in some purple veronicas and white daisies sprawled, drooping from the heat.

A cat was in a patch of sunlight, sitting on a rock to one side of the path.

It was a white cat, fur gleaming in the sun, so bright it hurt my eyes. The animal was so still I wouldn't have noticed it but for the bright, shining fur. As I watched, it lifted one paw and began to wash itself with quick flicks of its pink tongue.

There had been no signs inside the cottage of a cat. Perhaps it was a recent resident. Well, it looked healthy enough. If it wasn't being fed by someone, it was living quite well on what it could catch or forage in the area.

I climbed out of the car and collected my groceries. Dried twigs and leaves crunched under my feet, reminding me that it had been a dry summer, with little rain to mark the transition to autumn. Perhaps I should bestir myself enough to water some of the plants? I squeezed down the brick path between the wall of the cottage and the lush shrubs, brushing against something that smelt sweetly of vanilla.

The rock on which the cat had sat washing itself was now empty. The animal had gone as silently as it came. I felt a twinge of regret. I had never had a cat of my own, but I'd always admired their independence. A cat led its own life, coming and going when it pleased. A solitary animal. I sensed that a cat would suit me just perfectly.

I ate a leisurely lunch in the kitchen, and then

began to unpack my bags—last night I had pulled out my pyjamas and left the rest. I stowed most of the stuff in the wardrobe, tossing what remained into the two drawers of the dresser, and noticing as I did so that they were lined incongruously with old Disney comics. The speckled mirror caught my smile as I straightened.

Brown eyes, widely set in a pale face, and fair hair, usually cut very short, but now grown to my shoulders and curling untidily. It was an elfin face, a face I was used to seeing on film, television and in the glossy magazines. But suddenly it was a shock to see myself like this, so unguarded.

Had I altered at all, since Ian died? A little paler, perhaps, and a little thinner, but outwardly I was still Kate O'Hara, actor. It was inwardly that I felt like someone else. The energy and enthusiasm and ambition, the engine which had driven me, was gone. I was a stranger in the glittering world I had called home. Perhaps—the thought was like a heresy—I never had belonged there. And perhaps it had taken Ian's death to make me realise it.

Memories of the night of the crash and our argument tried to surface, but I pushed them firmly down. I took a deep breath. My eyes slid past my face, concentrating on the room behind me. The walls were painted a pale colour that may once have been pink. The plaster was uneven and chipped, and there were a couple of stains where rain had come in. Dust motes danced in the light and a cobweb hung in one corner, looking like antique lace.

I wondered whether I should find a broom and sweep it down, and then decided I liked it just the way it was.

The light on the river was changing as the sun swung around and the shadows lengthened. With a sudden determination, I found my pencils and went out onto the verandah. I sat down on the bricks with my feet on the grassy bank and my sketch book before me.

I had been a watercolourist ... *was* a watercolourist, I amended to myself. Nothing very special, nothing very talented, but I had enjoyed the challenge. Once, long ago, I had dreams of making a career of it. But then Ian had come into my life, the famous producer-director returned home from overseas triumphs, ready to impart his gems of wisdom to the students of the acting academy. I hadn't even decided whether acting was my 'thing', when he saw me and saw something in me that he could fashion to his own design. A bright spark that only needed fanning to shine. Kate O'Hara, actor.

And that was it. I was suddenly enmeshed in a world I had not known existed, and it was hard work, but it was exciting and I did shine, just as Ian said I would.

I sighed and looked down at my book.

Before I painted a picture, I usually made a light sketch, or a series of sketches and chose the best. It was so long since I had either sketched or painted, I found myself holding the pencil quite awkwardly, uncertain where to start. I made a few tentative strokes, trying to catch the flow of the river and the movement of air across it.

The final effect was far less than I had hoped for.

'Well, I'm no Van Gogh,' I sighed, and stretched my arms lazily.

The cat was about four metres from me, at the very edge of the river bank. I stopped, watching it. The animal was crouched, its body rigid with concentration, staring at some movement beneath the surface of the water. A fish? I wondered. I watched as it crept forward, head held so still, eyes fixed, whiskers bristling.

Something flapped overhead. I looked up and saw the bird from yesterday, gliding towards the middle of the river, preparing to make a landing. It did so with effortless efficiency, bobbing on the surface, the breeze barely ruffling its feathers. Smiling, I turned back to the cat to see how it was faring with its dinner, and discovered that once more it had vanished, quietly and completely.

Its disappearance left an odd sense of loss. The cat had been another solitary soul, like myself, and although it had not come close enough to stroke or speak to, I had felt the comfort of its company.

I shook my head. I had come here to be alone, to sort myself out, to think things through—all the old clichés.

And because I was frightened.

The fear rippled through me, just below my calm, like a tidal pull beneath the river's surface. Why was I afraid? What was I afraid of? I knew this was something I must look at squarely, and conquer. After Bolten had suggested my head-aches might be part of my feelings about Ian's death, there had been something in me that wanted to hide and pretend nothing was wrong. Overcoming that childish urge was one of the aims of this holiday.

The light on the river flickered. The bird rearranged its wings. I felt a wonderful sense of timelessness, and of peace. At this moment, I knew I could do anything.

'Anything? Well then,' I said grimly, 'let's deal with the stove!' And I stood up, brushed down the seat of my shorts and marched inside.

I woke in the darkness to the soft patter of rain on the roof.

I had been dreaming, but I didn't remember about what, only that it had been pleasant and soothing. The rain was so light it seemed to stroke the slate rather than fall upon it. I listened to the water dripping through a hole in the verandah roof outside my window, and the louder lapping of the river at the shore.

It sounded, almost, as if someone were rowing. I could make out the quiet, rhythmic pull of the oars in the water. I could picture the boat, a dark blur against the paler night sky, gliding towards the bank. As it drew closer, I could see a shape above the line of the bow, a dark shape with shoulders and head, arms pulling hard on the oars. And with each hard pull, the boat moved forward, silently, until it came up against the bank and stopped. The dark shape turned towards the cottage and was still. Watching. And then it began to climb out of the boat …

I started violently and sat up. The image had grown very real in my mind, so real that I imagined I really had heard the muffled sound of the bow striking the riverbank beyond my window. I listened again, intently, but now there was only the lap of the river and the drip on the verandah and the patter of the soft rain.

The next morning the rain kept me inside, and although it wasn't cold, it was chilly enough for me to hunt out a windcheater and jeans. Then I did something I hadn't done in a long time. I made a casserole to cook slowly in the oven of the wood stove.

Last night, after much swearing, I had managed to light the 'monster', as I had named it fondly. I had boiled the kettle, and heated up some frozen food from the general store. This morning I meant to do better than artificial flavourings and colourings. I couldn't live on mini pizzas and minute noodles for two weeks—well, not entirely. I would cook, and the monster wasn't going to stop me.

I relit the stove, letting it burn itself down to a slow, glowing heat before I placed the casserole in the oven. After a time the rich aroma of meat and vegetables began to waft through the cottage, making my mouth water. Suddenly enthusiastic, my sense of accomplishment soaring, I made a cake as well. No electricity meant I had to mix it by Kate-power, and I stirred until both arms ached.

The cake went into the oven with the casserole and I closed the door with a triumphant smile.

As I tidied up, my thoughts wandered. I wondered idly whether the white cat would return to share my meal. I imagined myself holding out a morsel, tempting it closer, close enough to touch. Where did the cat shelter in bad weather? Perhaps it was living in the garden, snug under the twisted branches of some overgrown shrub? Or perhaps it had a place beneath the verandah, far under the floorboards? Perhaps, even now, it lay there in the dusty darkness, listening to me moving around.

For no reason, I shivered.

I left the meal to cook itself, and went to find my cassette player. For most of the morning I listened to music, my feet stretched along the sofa, a book in front of me. But more often than not, I gazed out of the window, watching the play of the rain on the surface of the river. After a time I gave up pretending to read and took out my brushes and began to paint.

At various times in the past I had betrayed watercolours and dabbled with oils and acrylics. But I had always come back, repentant and more loyal than ever. There was something in the soft gentleness of them that suited me exactly.

The picture took shape more easily this time. I lost myself as I worked, the concentration of mind and body gave me a sense of serenity, of calm, that acting never did. Ian had always said that one day I would be up there with the greats … Hepburn, Streep and O'Hara! But I had never believed him, and I still didn't. I had been Ian's creation rather than my own. With him gone, the need to succeed had gone, too.

The painting was finished. I sat back to eye it critically. I quite liked the way I had captured the slant of the rain and the swirl of the water. But there was something not quite right about the river itself. I frowned, wondering how to improve it. Cautiously, using very light strokes of the brush, I filled in a shape on the water. It took form without my consciously guiding my hand —or so it seemed—until I realised I was painting a boat, with a man seated in it.

I sat back again. That was better. Or was it? With a sigh, knowing I would never be satisfied, I put the picture to one side. The casserole smelt good, and suddenly I was hungry.

The meal was delicious. I ate in the sitting

room, listening to music and the rain outside. Afterwards, my stomach pleasantly full, I persuaded myself I would feel better for a stroll outside.

The rain was only light, and I ignored it as I stepped down from the verandah and made my way towards the jetty. The wooden structure looked to be in poor condition, and by the giddy slant of the pylons, dangerously unstable. Some of them were rotten at the water line, and there were boards missing from the walkway. I didn't risk putting a foot on it, but instead stood and gazed over the river as the light faded in pale pinks and steely greys.

I wasn't looking for the cat. I had forgotten about it. And yet some part of my subconscious must have been watching and waiting, because when I saw the flash of white fur, my heart leapt with joy.

It was further along the riverbank, its long white shape moving through the wet grass. Steadily, keeping low, it was making its way up the slope towards the far wall of the cottage, where the old gum tree grew. I watched it crouch, and then run in a blur of pale colour. Once beside the tree, it sat and gazed about, very much at home, the white of its fur like a beacon in the gloom. It began to wash.

'Puss?' I tried tentatively, stooping and holding out my hand. 'Here, puss, puss?'

The cat stopped washing and stared at me fixedly. And then it simply turned and vanished.

Into the bushes, I told myself later. But at the time, it seemed as if the animal had vanished into thin air. One moment there, the next gone.

I guess I must have blinked, and missed the precise moment when it disappeared into the bushes. After all, it was almost dark. I simply missed it.

But when I returned to the cottage, I stared hard at the place where the white cat had been, as if I could somehow imagine it back again.

I again woke in the night, but this time there was no rain. It had stopped, and there was an eerie stillness to the place. Even the lap of the river seemed to have ceased. The air smelt damp and heavy, almost oppressive.

I had dreamed again, but this time the dream had an urgency to it, a disturbing restlessness that made me reluctant to return to sleep. And then the other memories came in, sweeping over me like a tidal wave, threatening to drown me.

I gave way and wept into my arms, my knees curled up to my chest, huddled into a ball of misery. I was a wife who had lost more than a husband; I had lost the reason for all I had done for the last five years. I was like a key without a door, and felt equally as useless.

Outside, water lapped, making a sound like oars being dipped and then dipped again. The old gum tree creaked like rowlocks and timber. A night bird called soft and low; a voice crying out something just beyond comprehension.

But I was crying for Ian, and I took no notice.

The morning brought an end to the rain.

The sun was shining again, bright and pragmatic. The emotional storm of the night had made me listless, with the beginnings of a pounding headache. I took some of Bolten's pain-killers and contemplated lying in bed for the day, staring at the wall. 'No,' I told myself. 'Not a good idea, Kate O'Hara.'

So I rose and went to tackle the monster for my morning cuppa.

After breakfast I collected my paints and equipment and settled myself on the verandah, propping one leg of my chair with a book to keep it steady on the wavey old brick paving. And then I lost myself in the intricacies of trying to capture the gleam of the morning light on the water and the ripple of the waves.

At lunchtime, I went in to fetch myself a sandwich and a cool drink, and stood in the doorway, eating and watching the river. It held a fascination for me, and I realised with some surprise that if I were to leave today I would already miss it.

After I had eaten, I wandered restlessly through the cottage, touching things, straightening things. And found myself standing before the fireplace in the sitting room, with its burden of dusty dried flowers, gazing up at the painting that hung above it.

I hadn't really examined it yet, apart from noting its darkness. That could be due either to the grime collected over the years or the darkening of the old varnish, which the artist had used to finish his picture. Or both!

I leaned closer, narrowing my eyes in an effort to see beyond age and dirt. The frame was rotten and had crumbled away at one corner, although the painting itself appeared to be in one piece. On impulse I reached up and took the whole thing down, carrying it to the window to give it my full attention.

At first I thought it was some European fantasy. A castle rising against a gloomy sky, with a lake in the foreground. But as I looked closer and tilted it towards the light, I saw the building was more modest than a castle, and the dark mass in the foreground was a river.

My river.

Excitement gripped me. I went outside, carrying the painting with me. It was easier to see in the full light of day. Time and dust had done their work, and yes, the varnish which had been layered so thickly over the paint had darkened, making it almost impossible to distinguish the true colours and whether it was supposed to be night or day. All the same, I could see now that it was indeed a river, my river, and the building in the background was the cottage, seeming to loom up on the riverbank.

It consisted of the same square, solid lines. There was a jetty, too, rather like the one there now, although in better condition. The old gum tree was straight and youthful, branches reaching towards the sky and forming an attractive frame for the upper part of the painting.

As a landscape it probably wasn't very exciting. Yet my hands trembled.

Leaning so close my nose almost touched the surface, I squinted into the dark river. There was a shape on the water. A shadow against the darkness. It was impossible to tell exactly what it was—yet I *knew*. I had painted the same thing myself, yesterday. It was a boat, and there was a man in it.

Slowly, as though afraid of what I might see, I turned the picture over. Nothing, but a stained, musty smelling piece of board that someone had used as backing. I peered again at the painting itself, this time at the perimeters. There was some writing at the very edge, where the frame had rotted away. Ignoring the uneasy feeling that I was vandalising someone else's property, I snapped the corner of the frame off.

The words were penned in black ink, making them nearly impossible to read. But, by holding the flat surface towards the sunlight and manoeuvring it, I found that the ink caught the light, whereas the painting remained dull. Laboriously, I traced each letter, frowning like a child spelling out its first word.

The Boatman. Nothing more. No artist, no date, no explanation.

'*The Boatman?*' I questioned aloud.

But my only answer was the slap of the river on the shore.

3

That night I slept dreamlessly. It was because of the tablets Bolten had given me, I knew that. They were to help me sleep, to help me stop worrying. I hadn't taken them before, but last night I had felt … well, that I needed them.

After breakfast, I shook off the fogginess of induced sleep and drove into Leeward to replenish my supplies. The town was awake, just. The woman in the general store blinked at me with tired eyes. 'Staying around here, are you?'

I was suddenly reluctant to answer. I felt as if

the cottage and the river were my private secret. But I told her what she wanted to know.

The woman smiled politely. 'Holiday, is it?'

'Sort of. I'm painting.'

The woman nodded, taking it in her stride. Her manner seemed to say: We get all sorts. 'I thought you might be here for the fishing. Get a few in for that this time of year.'

'Is there good fishing on the river?' I asked, my tone neutral.

The woman began to stack cartons of milk into a fridge. 'Not so much around Leeward. Most of the fishermen stay here, but they do their fishing further up the river, beyond the rapids.'

I nodded. Suddenly the dip of the oars and the hush of a boat on the water was very clear in my head. 'I thought I heard a boat one night. Maybe it was someone fishing.'

The woman smiled again, her eyes brightening. 'You're staying at the cottage on Devlin's Stretch!' she guessed.

'Devlin's Stretch?'

The woman nodded. 'There's a bit of history to that place, love. Devlin was a boatman, and he lived there in the old days. That part of the river is still called Devlin's Stretch, after him.'

'Devlin was a boatman?' I breathed. Well, that explained the painting in the sitting room. A bit of local history turned into cash for some budding artist!

The woman was ringing up my purchases. 'Maybe what you heard was his ghost,' she said pleasantly. 'That'll be nine dollars and forty-five cents.'

'Pardon?'

'Nine dollars and forty-five cents.'

'No.' I fumbled with the money, placing it into the steady, waiting palm. 'What did you mean, his ghost?'

The woman's eyes sparkled in a way that led me to think she didn't take the ghost story very seriously. 'They say it's the ghost of someone in a boat, rowing on the river. But it'd have to be Devlin, wouldn't it? Who else?' She shrugged and began to tidy some chocolate bar displays. 'I don't believe in ghosts myself.'

'Someone in a boat,' I repeated, and a shiver galloped up my spine at the idea of a ghostly boatman rowing around on *my* river. Was that what I had heard? And then my commonsense re-asserted itself—Ian always said I lacked imagination. 'No, I don't believe it. What I heard was just a fisherman.'

'Don't worry, I reckon you're right. That, or the water stirring around. If you start thinking about ghosts you'll scare yourself silly.' She gave me a searching look. 'But you seem like a sensible girl.'

I gave her back a weak smile.

'Have I seen you somewhere before?' she asked suspiciously. 'You look familiar.'

'No, I don't think so,' I lied firmly.

The woman considered me a moment longer and then shrugged. 'Oh well, we get all sorts here.'

The white cat was there when I got back to the cottage. I stopped the car and sat, watching it, as I had done before. It was sitting on the same rock, cleaning its face with a thoroughness that was commendable.

Devlin's Stretch, I thought, going over my newfound knowledge with a certain relish. Devlin the boatman.

I didn't know whether to laugh or be intrigued, or both. I had heard a boat, I was certain of it … or was I? Perhaps it had been the wind? It was easy to doubt, after the event. And in such a quiet place as this, it would be easy to begin to imagine … things. It must have been a fisherman.

'Well, which is it, the wind or a fisherman?' I asked myself impatiently.

The cat looked up at the sound of my voice. It had yellow eyes, and for a moment they gazed steadily into mine. And then the animal stepped neatly off the rock and wandered away into the tangled garden.

'Exactly as it did the other night,' I told myself with a laugh. 'Only it was too dark to see properly.'

Another mystery solved.

I made myself a snack and carried it on to the verandah. Afterwards, I manoeuvred out one of the chairs from the kitchen, and set up my easel and my materials. The river was still shadowy and secret, and I was determined to capture its mood.

I began to work, forgetting everything else in my urge to create something of the river and the light, and perhaps myself. I worked throughout the morning and late into the afternoon, breaking briefly for a snack. By the time I had finished it was close to darkness, and my nose was only centimetres from the paper.

But I was pleased with myself.

I stretched my fingers and then my arms, holding them out before me and smiling. Across the water, the evening bird circled and found a place to land. A gust of wind ruffled the surface and fanned the bird's feathers.

I realised, with a shiver, that it had grown colder. The river was dark now, a flowing, shapeless shadow. Quickly I gathered up my things and retreated into the cottage to light the stove and a candle and prepare my meal.

I didn't think of the boatman, not until I saw the painting still lying on the kitchen table where I had left it. Carefully, I replaced it in the sitting room, resolving to have a go at the varnish if I had time. The Tucks would surely appreciate my restoring their work of art to its former glory, especially as I had broken a piece off the frame.

Outside the wind was rising, rattling the leaves of the gum tree and making a branch tap against the guttering. I could hear the river, louder tonight, slapping at the bank. It had begun to sound as if it might be a wild night.

Had Devlin sat here on such nights?

The thought came unbidden, and I stopped

what I was doing, startled by it. Well, he probably had, I told myself tartly. He had probably sat much as I was, eating his meal, preparing for bed, thinking of what needed to be done in the morning.

I wondered what he had looked like, this Devlin, but my mind stayed strangely blank. With a shrug, I took my candle and climbed into bed.

I had brought a novel with me, but it failed to hold my attention. KGB agents were all very well in their place, but their plots and counterplots seemed outlandish here, in the old cottage by the river. My thoughts began to drift.

At last, exasperated, I set the book aside and blew out the candle. 'Good night,' I murmured into the darkness, and then wondered why I had.

I woke later to the sensation of being watched. When I opened my eyes, it was to see the pale blurred form of the white cat sitting on the end of my bed. It stared at me a moment, silently, and began to wash its face. Half asleep still, the slow, measured movements mesmerised me, until my eyelids fluttered and closed again.

I made myself a substantial breakfast. 'If this keeps up,' I told the kettle, 'I'll have to buy new clothes.'

But I knew I could afford to put on some weight, and I was feeling better than I had for a long time. The fresh air and the quiet were doing me good. Even Ian hadn't spoken to me for a while.

After breakfast I took out my painting equipment and set off along the riverbank to try and discover where the local artist had made his painting of the boatman.

I had examined the painting again that morning, holding it up to the light. It was desperately in need of cleaning, so badly I had decided I didn't want to meddle with it in case I stripped off the paint as well as the varnish. I wondered whether someone in Leeward would be able to do the job for me.

After a bit of trial and error, I found the spot, or near enough. There was a slight curve in the river and one tree, braver than the rest, had taken root right on the waterline. It was here that the unknown artist had set up his or her easel.

I leaned against the smooth trunk of the tree and scanned the scene. I could do a similar painting—probably better! I smiled at my own arrogance. I could call it *The Ghostly Boatman.*

Or Devlin, Ian mocked.

I went still. Suddenly a sort of revulsion rose in me. 'Why don't you leave me alone?' I burst out. 'You're dead!'

This time Ian said nothing, and maybe that was worse.

Slowly, disheartened now, I wandered back with my painting gear to the cottage, the river lapping beside me.

After a morning spent doing very little, I gave up and found my purse and car keys, and hefted the old painting out to the car.

The woman in the general store greeted me like an old friend. She seemed to regard my question as a challenge. 'You could try Linda Kearns in the craft shop,' she said. 'If she can't do it, she'll know who can. Plenty of arty folk around Leeward.'

It sounded like an insult, but I pretended not to notice.

'No more ghosts?' the woman asked, as I left.

I laughed and shook my head. 'No more ghosts.'

Linda Kearns was a young fifty, with dangly gold earrings, a gypsy blouse and a long red skirt. She looked at me with interest while I explained my mission.

'I *can* help you as it happens,' she replied. 'My son does oils, and a bit of restoration work on the side. I'll take it home to him … if that's all right?' Perhaps she had caught my uncertain look.

'It doesn't belong to me,' I explained. 'I wouldn't want anything to happen to it.'

Linda pursed her lips. 'I'm sure it would be

all right. Look, I'll give him a ring and ask him.
Can you hang on a moment?'

I nodded, and wandered around the shop
while Linda made her call in soft tones. There
were embroidered cushion covers and cleverly
painted bookends, as well as everything imagin-
able with 'Greetings from Leeward' stamped on
it. The ceiling was hung with windchimes of
every description, and several intricate American
Indian dreamcatchers.

'It's all right,' Linda called out, interrupting
my inspection. 'He says he can do it over the next
week, maybe sooner.'

'That will be fine. I'm leasing a cottage on the
river. Devlin's Stretch, I think they call it.'

Linda nodded. The name obviously meant
nothing to her, and I breathed a sigh of relief. I'd
had about all I could take of ghost stories. 'I'm
here every day,' Linda said with a friendly smile.
'Call in next time you're in Leeward and I can tell
you when it'll be ready.'

I thanked her again and went outside. A
couple of cars passed through the town, barely
slowing down on their way somewhere. That was
probably how most people saw Leeward—a blur
of colour, to be got through as quickly as possible. But I walked slowly, enjoying the sensation
of the sun on my face and the rustle of the dry
leaves along the footpath.

Autumn had always been my favourite
season. As a child I had enjoyed rolling in the
leaves, or mounding them over myself and

jumping out of them, breathless with laughter and excitement. I wondered suddenly, painfully, why Ian and I had not had children. But I already knew the answer. Too busy pursuing my career. Ian would have been a good father, I told myself loyally, squirming at the memory of my earlier shouting at the voice in my head.

A sign board stood on the path before me. I blinked, taking it in. 'Leeward Museum. 9 to 5, Monday to Saturday, $2 adults, $1 children.'

I looked up. The museum was actually an old house, set in a side street, and painted in heritage colours. Woolly dahlias and shasta daisies waved to the sun along the path to the front door. I hesitated, but I had nothing else to do, and my painting mood seemed to have deserted me. I set off towards the open door.

There was a visitors' book in the hall, full of the comments of school children trying to be funny. A case of stuffed animals watched me as I passed.

The first room had been set out with long tables covered in books and photographs of Leeward worthies. Glass cases held more treasured relics, each carefully labelled in faded ink. Here were the lengths of chain and rusted iron balls, pitiful yet grim remnants of the convict era. Someone had donated a sword that belonged to a grandfather who had fought in the Boer War. There was also a photograph of the gentleman in uniform, looking suitably fearless. A couple of manikins posed woodenly in the clothing of an earlier period, their hairstyles more 1960s than 1860s.

I felt the presence behind me half a second before I saw the reflection in the glass case, and spun around with a start to face the old man. He hesitated, eyeing me uneasily. Perhaps, I thought, amused, he had thought me part of the exhibit.

'Are you interested in anything in particular?' he asked diffidently, careful not to intrude or offend.

I took a breath. 'I'm sorry. I was just looking. You have quite a collection.'

It sounded glib, but the old man smiled, pleased to chat. I supposed it must get rather lonely in the Leeward Museum during the off-season.

'Lot of history in Leeward,' he replied. 'People don't realise unless they stop and take a look.'

'I suppose it's the same in most small towns.'

But the old man didn't want to admit that Leeward was the same as anywhere else. 'You just passing through?' he asked, interest sparking in his pale blue eyes.

Here we go again, I thought, and took a breath. 'I'm leasing a cottage by the river. I believe it's called Devlin's Stretch, or so the woman in the general store tells me. She also tells me it's supposed to be haunted.'

He grinned. 'That's Mrs Fildrew, and I can imagine what she said. Well, don't let that worry you. I've been out that way many times fishing and I've never seen anything more ghostly than the mist on the water.' He tapped his cheek with one gnarled finger. 'I reckon we've got a photo of the cottage somewhere. It was taken late last century, but I don't think the place has changed much since it was built. Do you want to see it?'

I followed him into another room, and made my way around an enormous pianola and a couple of tapestry covered chairs, incongruously arranged with a mangle and wash tub. A stuffed owl sat high on a bookcase, staring down at us with beady, unblinking eyes.

The old man had paused in front of another glass case, and I came to stand beside him. He pointed. 'That's it, there. Used to be a boatman's cottage in the old days. That's a ferryman,' he added. 'Someone who ferried folk from one side of the river to the other, for a fee. Never was a proper punt there. Never enough traffic to justify it, I suppose.'

I hadn't realised that 'boatman' had a meaning other than a man who owned a boat, or fished from a boat. My head felt as if it were stuffed full of cotton wool; I gave the owl a sympathetic glance.

The old man was still talking, and I noticed he had a name tag pinned to the pocket of his shirt: 'Jim Wallace'.

'That part of the river was a crossing place early in the piece, before Leeward was even settled. Then the convicts were brought in to build the road.' He glanced sideways at me. 'That was in the 1820s and 1830s, when they decided to build a proper road from Hobart to Launceston —it was just a track before then. The old roads in Tasmania are all convict built, you know.'

Convicts, I thought with a sigh. I supposed one couldn't delve very far back into Tasmanian history, indeed into Australian history, without turning them up in droves.

'The convict camp was just a bit north of where you're staying. There was a quarry there and a barracks for the men. They used to cart the stone every morning to wherever they were working on the road. There was talk of a causeway, too, or a bridge across the river. But there was never enough traffic then to justify that either. Most of the traffic was on this side, the Leeward side.

'The quarry's been filled in now, but you can still see what's left of the barracks. There's a signpost on the highway, and a track into the bush. There were thirty or forty men there at one time.'

He knew it off by heart.

'I read something about a fire on a sign,' I said. 'What happened, was someone smoking in bed?'

It was meant to be a joke, but Mr Wallace gave me a quelling look. History isn't a joke to these people, I reminded myself uneasily. They live and breathe it. Take it easy, Kate. You don't want to upset the old dear.

'The fire was deliberately set,' Mr Wallace said stonily. 'The convicts got out that night, so it was probably them who set it. Could have been pretty nasty, but it just so happened Major Dunwich was doing an inspection tour of the roadworks—he was one of the top men overseeing the building of the roads in Van Diemen's Land at the time. He was staying overnight at the barracks. It was Dunwich who took charge. The convicts were all rounded up again quick smart and no-one was hurt. Fortunately.'

'Yes, yes, of course.' I put as much feeling as I could into those murmured words, and was rewarded with a small smile from Mr Wallace.

'Devlin was the boatman in those days,' he went on, thawing some more. 'The rumour went that he had something to do with the fire, but no-one ever got to the bottom of it. No-one ever could, because Devlin disappeared afterwards. Never seen again.'

'Well!' I smiled. 'It's certainly a wonderful story.'

'There's a contemporary account of Leeward around that time which contains details of the fire at the convict barracks. The book was reprinted by the Leeward Museum last year.' Mr Wallace looked proud of himself. 'A hundred copies sold. Can I interest you in one, Mrs … eh?'

'O'Hara,' I murmured with a weak smile. 'Kate.'

He seemed to take that for a 'yes', and went off in search of the book. I stood and gazed at the photograph.

No, nothing much had changed. The cottage

looked the same as it did now, apart from the jetty. That was new, evidently.

'Here we are!' Mr Wallace returned, the thin, bound volume held triumphantly aloft. 'It's an account written by one of our early pioneers. He was only a lad at the time of the fire. Devlin is mentioned in it.'

That sparked my interest. I took the book from him with a smile. It was called *Boyhood Recollections*, a harmless enough title, and the author was one Howard Tuck, Esq. I liked the 'Esquire', and wondered whether Howard Tuck was an ancestor of Bob Tuck, whose family owned my cottage.

'Thank you. How much does it cost?'

My smile didn't falter when he told me, but I suddenly understood how it was that a small place like Leeward could afford such a comprehensive museum.

The light was fading by the time I reached the cottage. There was a pleasant smell of eucalyptus in the air. I walked slowly along the path to the front door, enjoying the feel of the sinking sun on my back. The cat was nowhere in sight. Vaguely, I recalled dreaming of it last night, but the dream was too blurred for me to remember properly. Hadn't it been sitting on my bed or some such thing? The thought touched a chord of unease in me.

The door opened with its usual silence, and I stepped inside. The air smelt warm and pleasant, with a mingling of casserole, candles and wood smoke.

It smelt like home.

Before dawn I woke, the throbbing in my head a warning of what was to come. I stumbled from my bed and into the kitchen, where I gulped down some of Bolten's pain-killers. I crept back to bed and closed my eyes, ignoring the lurching in my stomach.

By noon the headache had still not gone, and I had taken my prescribed dose of the tablets, and more. The pounding in my head went on, violent and unremitting. The world about me appeared to vibrate, as if a giant were jumping up and down.

CHAPTER FOUR

It had never been this bad before. It was as if the headaches in Melbourne had been but a dress rehearsal, and now I had the real thing.

I went to bed early; I could do nothing else. Outside the sky and river turned pink and mauve, the evening so soft and pretty I could have wept for the lost opportunity to capture it with my paints. As I tossed back the bedclothes, something slid off the bed and onto the floor with a thump.

Perhaps Howard Tuck would distract me from my pain. I picked up *Boyhood Recollections* and tried to read.

Soon I sighed and, tossing the book aside, blew out the candle. I squeezed my eyes shut, but coloured lights danced behind my lids, on and off, like malevolent Christmas trees.

'Ho, ho, ho,' I muttered.

My voice echoed strangely in the dark silence. I became aware of the quiet. Nothing was stirring, not even the leaves on the old gum tree. The air had that chill that warns of frost.

Focus, Kate, for God's sake!

The words came from nowhere, unbidden. Ian's words. The words he uttered whenever he had felt I was glancing off to the side—and I was always glancing off to the side!—losing that direct, forward, merciless gaze he had himself. He had been a hard taskmaster, but it had paid off. Without Ian I would never have got where I did. Talent wasn't enough, not really. You had to have the drive to go with it.

'I should be grateful,' I said aloud.

But I wasn't. The emotions inside me erupted, making my head throb viciously. I felt guilty that I had been driving the car the night Ian died, and that we had argued ... Suddenly, through the pain, I realised something that until now I had not been able, or had not wanted, to face.

I was relieved.

An awful, unforgivable sense of relief that Ian was dead. And everything that being his wife, his creation, had meant was finished too. I was Kate O'Hara, nobody, again. And it had taken Ian's death to make me realise how much I had loathed what I had become.

Strangely, now that I'd faced this truth, the headache began to ease. As loud, unwelcome knocking on a door stops when the messenger is allowed to enter. The revelation held me spellbound, and I may have lain brooding over it indefinitely had something not distracted me.

There was a small sound outside. A movement on the river. As I listened it came again, the sound of oars dipping into the water and slipping out again, the muffled thump of rowlocks turning. It was a boat, coming closer.

Oddly, my immediate reaction was anger. I didn't want to be disturbed. How dare someone go fishing at this time of night! And then the anger went, and I smiled at myself. The river was my exclusive property, was it? No fishing allowed on Devlin's Stretch while Kate O'Hara is in residence!

The boat was definitely drawing closer. I could hear the dip of the oars quite plainly now, and the rattle of the rowlocks. A voice called out, softly. A man's voice. It drifted away across the water, into silence.

For a minute there was nothing, and then I heard the thud of the bow striking the riverbank, and the bump and thump of the oars being pulled in, every sound magnified by the stillness. Whoever was in the boat climbed out. I heard the scuff of his boots on the grass, and the dragging sound the hull made as he heaved the boat further up the bank to secure it. Silence again, and then the scuff of boots grew louder, nearer. He was coming towards the cottage.

What was this?

I sat bolt upright in bed, and now my heart was banging hard.

It was all very well for someone to be fishing out on the river, but it was another matter for that someone to be coming to visit me in the middle of the night!

A hundred scenarios replayed in my mind, movies I had seen, movies I had acted in, all ending in gory murder. I swallowed and reminded myself that I was not the nervous type. Perhaps whoever was out there had left a car up on the highway and was just using the cottage as a right of way to get back to it. Perhaps he had done it before, when the cottage was empty, and didn't realise it was currently being leased.

I had talked myself so thoroughly into that scenario, that the sound of heavy footsteps on the verandah came as an even greater shock. A shadow passed by the dark square of my window. I waited, tense and silent, for the knock to sound on my door. There was none. Instead I heard a rattle as the knob turned, and then the creak of the heavy door swinging open.

I had locked it! The words flashed through my panic-stricken brain. I know I locked it! Does he have a key? And then, with a flooding wave of relief: It must be the caretaker. Only he would have a key. He must think the cottage is still empty!

The floor groaned as my uninvited guest stepped inside. With him came a gust of cold air and the smell of the river. I saw a shadow pass my doorway. A big, black mass that had no shape, no definition. Yet I sensed his glance towards me as I sat rigid in my bed. Then his footsteps carried him on, moving towards the back of the cottage, into silence.

Outside, it began to rain.

What do I do now? I asked myself, and shivered violently. Do I get up and make him a cup of tea, whoever he is? The idea was repellent and frightening. Slowly, toes curling on the cold, hard boards of the floor, I climbed out of bed, collected my torch from the drawer, and went to peer into the passage.

There was no light and no movement. It felt empty. My fingers tightened on the torch but I didn't want to turn it on yet. I didn't want to give my position away. Suddenly the darkness had become my friend.

Inch by inch, I crept out of my doorway and turned towards the front door. It was closed. I looked the other way. Nothing but darkness and silence. Panic clutched at me, squeezing the air out of my chest, and I stood, not knowing what to do. Just as the panic threatened to overwhelm me, the ridiculousness of the whole thing freed me.

'Look, I don't know what you think you're playing at,' I said loudly in a brisk voice, my best 'I'm in control of this situation' voice. 'I'm leasing the cottage at the moment, and I'd appreciate it if you'd leave.'

Silence. Nothing.

'Did you hear me? I want you to leave, now.'

Anger replaced panic, and I switched on the torch. The bright light was surprisingly comforting. With the torch held firmly before me in one hand and my sturdy wooden hair brush in the other, I continued my search through the house.

The sitting room was empty. Cautiously, fingers tightening on the handle of the brush, I went towards the bathroom. It was shadowy but it, too, was empty. That left the kitchen. I took a deep breath and swung the beam of the torch wildly into the room, expecting at any moment to have it knocked from my fingers. But there was no-one there. I hesitated, at a loss. There appeared to be no-one in the cottage apart from myself.

It took a moment to accept this. I knew there was no other way out, but I searched the whole cottage again. And again. It was definitely empty. Frowning now, relief giving way to puzzlement, I returned to the front door and turned the knob. It was locked, just as it had been when I went to bed. It had always been locked.

'I must have dreamed it all,' I said aloud, trying to keep my voice steady. But I knew I hadn't, and the alternatives were so monstrous, so frightening, I hardly knew how to face them.

I sat on my bed and set the torch down with a shaking hand. Bolten had said nothing about the possibility of hallucinations! Surely headaches and hallucinations were two entirely separate things? Sometimes, when the headaches were at their worst, I had experienced blurred vision, darkness at the edge of my sight ... but nothing had ever *appeared* to me. Yet there was no other explanation.

Well, there was one, but that was so unbelievable as to be totally ... unbelievable!

'Devlin?' I whispered the name. It seemed to hang suspended in the darkness about me.

The rain had gone by the morning. The sun shone down on Devlin's Stretch. I lay in bed and felt myself question what I had heard and seen and felt. I did not want to accept it had happened. I wanted to believe it was some previous lessee or the caretaker who had stumbled on the cottage, thinking it empty, and decided to take shelter. And who, finding the place already inhabited, had simply slipped away.

'Slipped away. Right,' I muttered as I climbed out of bed. Birds were singing in the gum tree and I heard the drone of an aeroplane, far away. Outside my bedroom door, the sunlight was pouring through the Roman blinds in the sitting room, pooling like melted butter on the floor. The imprint of the boot was quite plain, and inarguable.

It was dry now, but I could see it had been damp and muddy. It was a large imprint for a large boot, and probably a large man wearing it.

So there really had been someone here last night!

My eyes moved, following the prints to their origin, at the front door. They went past my own bedroom door and on, towards the kitchen and bathroom at the back of the cottage. Exactly as I would have expected them to go, judging by the sounds last night.

Slowly, full of an uneasy excitement, I followed them. Perhaps there was a secret door —a way out I had somehow failed to notice. But the bootprints ended at the back wall of the kitchen. Simply ended. As though whoever had walked through the cottage had walked straight through a solid stone wall. And it was solid, because I ran my hands over it, and even gave it a few good thumps with my fists. The cottage might have been old and primitive, but it wasn't about to fall down for at least another hundred years.

No-one made of flesh and blood could walk through a wall. But then again, surely a hallucination did not leave footprints?

I sat down on one of the kitchen chairs, my legs suddenly giving way. So what did that leave? Ghosts? Did ghosts leave footprints? I seemed to remember reading things about bloodstains that couldn't be removed, bloody handprints, the indentation of a head on a pillow where no-one had slept. But muddy bootprints? It tested my credulity.

I groaned and put my hands over my face. Maybe I should give Bolten a ring? I was fairly certain, if I did, he would insist I come home immediately so that he could run more tests. I had had enough tests. This was my time alone, my time to come to terms with what I was and what I had done with my life, to look to my future. I wouldn't have it cut short, and certainly not by Devlin!

The critical part of my mind caught up with my emotions. Hang on there, it said. Why Devlin? Assuming this was no hallucination, which was a big ask, why should it be Devlin? There are more things in heaven and earth, as the man said.

'Devlin,' I repeated stubbornly, and suddenly remembered the book Jim Wallace had sold me at the museum. I would have to read it. There was always the possibility that hidden within its tedious pages was something to shed light on what was happening to me. If it was Devlin who had come haunting, then there had to be a reason.

There was always a reason.

Howard Tuck was as boring as I had remembered from my attempt to read him last night. But I persevered, drinking coffee to keep myself awake after my restless night.

Howard's father had taken up land at Leeward and his mother had born five strong sons, all of them prime examples of colonial manhood. There were more descriptions of tree felling and sheep doctoring than I cared to read, interspersed with mentions of other Leeward worthies. Colonel Seers was one of them, a Waterloo veteran settled on the land, and another was James Haydon, a ship's surgeon retired to sheep farming. The owner of the inn and local den of iniquity was Iziah Ducat, and his wife's name was Janey, her nickname 'Grandma' giving a fair indication of her appearance. There were others, but I didn't think they had much bearing on my own investigation. Finally, after pages of wattle and daub cottages with leaky roofs, disputed land boundaries, and the perfidies of convict servants,

I came upon one Major Dunwich, a very important officer and close friend of Governor Arthur. He possessed, according to Howard Tuck, Esq., 'most gentlemanly manners' and presented a 'particularly fine figure in his uniform'. Howard, I sighed, was rather impressed by a nice uniform. He mentioned them regularly, and was always sure to watch the soldiers drilling when he visited Hobart or 'The Camp', as he called it affectionately. Major Dunwich was an acquaintance of Howard's father, and heavily into building roads all over the colony.

I yawned.

A few pages later, there was something of more immediate interest. I sat up in my chair and blinked.

Devlin was the local boatman. A giant of a man, and dark of visage. He lived alone in his cottage by the river and seemed to wish it no other way. The mothers of Leeward were known to threaten their disobedient children that Devlin would come after them, take them into his boat and row them away into the night, from whence they would never return. Of course, my brothers and myself never required such treatment, being well brought-up to those responsibilities which are a pleasure to dutiful sons.

'Smug pig,' I retorted savagely. And then read it again, more carefully. A giant of a man. Dark of visage. Was that what Devlin looked like? A pity it didn't say what size boots he took, I mocked myself with a smile. But nevertheless my heart began to thud.

There were some more items of interest further on, hidden amongst the tedium of Howard's days.

> *The convicts were housed in cells in a large barracks, and turned out every morning to begin work at six. The iron gang consisted of felons sent to work upon it from one to twelve months, depending on the severity of the offence. They were, many of them, the most degraded wretches, while others were so ashamed of the state in which they found themselves they could hardly hold one's gaze, not even the gaze of a little lad such as myself.*
>
> *The overseer was Duncan Cromarty, a brutal man, of whom the convicts were in terror. It was rumoured he flogged them every day and twice on Sundays. Whatever the truth, there was not a hint of trouble from them until July 1829.*
>
> *During this period, there was at the convict barracks an incident. A fire started in one of the cells, and spread quickly to the rest of the building. The convicts were turned out in order to save their unworthy lives while the flames were extinguished by the soldiers and those of the felons who could be persuaded to assist. It was afterwards rumoured that the fire had*

been started by some misguided friend or sympathiser of one of the convicts, to enable him to escape. And indeed, several did escape during the melee. They were, thankfully, speedily recaptured by their guards. Major Dunwich, who was at the time inspecting the work on the roads, and had stayed overnight at the barracks, swiftly took charge. All Leeward should be grateful to him, for if (dreadful thought!) the convicts had been allowed to roam free, many civilian lives may have been lost.

Was control really so quickly and easily restored? I couldn't believe it. With men running everywhere in the dark and the fire blazing, it would have been a shambles. And were the convicts really all rounded up, or did a few slip off, never to be found? That was an interesting thought, but I doubted it. The authorities would have had to admit they'd fouled up. Runaway convicts were not known for their good manners and kindness to settlers in the lonely bush. Everyone would need to be warned, and quickly.

I returned to Howard.

But the military were not the only heroes of the fire. The boatman, Devlin, had seen the flames from his cottage and swiftly arrived on the scene. Devlin saved several lives in the blaze; he was reported to have dragged some felons, faint from the smoke, to safety. So why, immediately afterwards, did he vanish, never to be seen again? There was a rumour that he had run off like a fleeing convict, to live wild in the bush, but why would he sacrifice livelihood and freedom for such a venture? Another rumour stated that he had returned to Ireland with a fortune in gold he had found during the fire, but this is just nonsensical.

Well, I thought, I agree with you there, Howard! But Howard had not yet finished his say.

As to the truth of the matter, that is something Devlin wanted to remain a mystery, and I have kept my promise to leave it so.

I slammed the book down angrily. What the hell did that mean? Whatever the answer to the mystery of Devlin's disappearance, I had had enough of Howard Tuck. The weather was still fine, I noted, glancing out of the window, and I might as well make the most of it!

I painted during much of the afternoon, concentrating on that and purposely excluding all other thoughts. A chill wind blew across the water, but I worked on, desperate to capture the fading light on the water as evening approached. Finally a splatter of rain brought me to my senses, and gasping, I grabbed up my gear and ran for the cottage.

Within moments the rain was pounding on the roof, so loud I felt deafened. Outside, the river was hidden in the grey sheet of the downpour. The gum tree twisted and danced in the gusts of wind.

Laughing, I found a towel and began to dry myself, at the same time peering out of the window at the storm. Inside it was dark, but outside it was darker. It shouldn't have been nightfall for another hour yet, but it was doubtful there'd be a return to daylight now. The storm had seen to that.

I went from room to room with the torch, checking for leaks. The only one I found was in the bathroom. I searched out the biggest bowl from the kitchen cupboard and set it under the drip. Then I lit the stove and began to prepare my evening meal.

Outside the storm raged on. Every now and then gusts of wind and rain would hammer the side of the cottage, like angry fists demanding admittance. But the old cottage had withstood many a gale in its lifetime, and it wasn't about to admit defeat now. I felt quite safe. Which was a little strange, perhaps, when I allowed myself to remember what had happened the previous night.

I thought about it while I ate.

Despite my fear and confusion, there had been one important thing missing when it came to Devlin's visit—at least I presumed it was

Devlin. I hadn't felt threatened. I hadn't felt as if he meant to harm me. There had been no sense of deadly danger or evil. Whatever it was that passed by my door in the darkness, it had done me no harm, and I felt certain it had not intended any.

Indeed, the atmosphere of the cottage was not one of foreboding, but one of welcome. It was as if ... as if Devlin wanted me here. I could feel him now, a rippling shadow in the corner of my mind. It was as if he were waiting. But for what?

I had hoped to find some clues in Howard Tuck's book, if not to why Devlin's ghost haunted the cottage, then clues about the man himself. But so far I had learnt very little from Howard about the boatman. He was a hero, it seemed, who had promptly vanished. Most heroes like to stick around and soak up some of the glory, but not Devlin. Perhaps he was just shy?

I knew I should read further, but couldn't bring myself to pick up the book. I'd had enough of Howard. When it was time to go to bed, I hesitated over the sleeping tablets Bolten had given me. If I took them, I would sleep through to morning and nothing would disturb me, short of an earthquake and even then! But if I took them ... I would never know if he came back.

And if he does? I asked myself grimly. What then?

I set the tablets aside without taking them, and settled myself in bed to read a chapter or two of my KGB novel. The candle flame danced, sensitive to a draught from the old window. Outside, the storm had dwindled into steady rain, and the sound of it on the roof was very soothing.

I closed my eyes, still listening. I hadn't been mistaken about the cottage. It welcomed me, it wrapped its arms around me, it said, 'Stay here, Kate O'Hara and you'll not be sorry, stay here with Devlin.'

The candle burned on, low now, a mere flicker of yellow light. Outside, the rain eased and the river slipped by and a possum scurried across the roof, seeking its supper. I didn't mean to fall asleep, but my body was so tired that sleep caught me unawares, taking me down.

The noise of the boat was soft at first, the gentle dipping of the oars far away. I heard it in my dreams and was lulled by it. But as it drew closer the sound grew louder, and I awoke, confused and disorientated. The candle was almost out, wax piled like white worms around the stub.

Then I heard the boat again. The bow came to rest against the riverbank with a thud. My heart seemed to stop and then start again, banging in my chest as if it meant to leap right out. Boots, muffled at first by the wet grass, scraped across the verandah. A large dark shadow passed my window.

'Oh no.' I meant to whisper the words, but no sound came out.

Creaking, the door opened, and there was a sharp smell of rain and the river and something more I couldn't distinguish. Something bitter-sweet and half-forgotten. The matt darkness of the passage beyond my open doorway stirred as though taking shape, melding itself into something of density and form. I saw a hand, blunt fingered, and then a wrist and the sleeve riding above it. My eyes moved upward, quite beyond my control, and a face came out of the black in a series of planes and hollows. A man's face.

Devlin's face.

He was so tall he had to stoop to see under the door's lintel, and his face was twisted with some feeling I didn't understand but which caught at me like a cat's claws. His lips parted as if he wanted to speak ... as if he desperately wanted to say something to me. But the effort was too great, and he was fading back into the shadows. His eyes, dark and melancholy, held mine. And then he was gone.

I lay, shocked, my breath rasping in my ears. A giant of a man, Howard Tuck had said, and dark of visage. I knew I had just seen Devlin—or whatever was left of the man who had been Devlin. He had been like a dark angel, but with such sadness in him. I had wanted to put my arms about him and comfort him. Whatever the cost.

I lay in bed and watched the sun filter through the window.

After my experience last night, I had slept well. The shadow that was Devlin had not returned, and again I had felt quite certain he meant me no harm. I was afraid, yes, so afraid my teeth chattered. But it was not fear of what Devlin might do to me.

I was positive now that it was him. I no longer needed local legend or gossip or Howard Tuck's 'recollections'. Devlin had not gone from this place. He was here, searching or waiting for ... something. And my fear was laced with a great sadness for him and an even greater need to solve the mystery and set him free.

You're behaving irrationally, Kate! Ring Bolten. Tell him what's happening.

Ian's voice slid slyly into my mind, but I ignored it. I didn't want to ring Bolten, I didn't want him to order me back to Melbourne. I loved this place. But it was more than that. I didn't want Bolten telling me that I was seeing things that weren't really there.

Suddenly it was very important to me that Devlin not be just a figment of an ill mind.

I made breakfast and carried it out onto the verandah. I had just begun to eat, when I heard the engine. Startled, I walked to the side of the cottage and stood, watching, as the shiny red of the car flashed briefly through the trees, vanished, and then reappeared at the turning circle. It drew up with a spurt of earth, and above the ticking of the cooling engine, I could hear voices.

Oh God.

Dixie and Cecil! I had worked with Dixie on *The Lost Ones*. We had got on well, but ... there was always a 'but' with Dixie. She was a bit overwhelming, a bit like Ian, and if she was overwhelming in the hustle and bustle of the city, how would she seem here at Devlin's Stretch?

'Kate!' The high, carrying voice shattered the tranquillity. A bird crashed up through the branches of a tree and flew off. Out of the corner of my eye, I thought I caught a glimpse of something white, running.

'Kate.' Cecil was quieter, his crooked smile offering an apology for the intrusion. I knew this visit would not have been his idea.

But it would never have occurred to Dixie that she was unwelcome, she was that sort of person. She charged forward now, all blonde streaks and designer jeans. Dixie prided herself on pursuing life rather than letting it come to her.

'I'm down here doing a play in Hobart and I was talking with Jack on the phone and he said you were here, too!' she was saying. 'How amazing! We had to come and catch up!'

Jack, I sighed. He was the producer on *The Lost Ones*, and the one person, apart from Bolten, whom I had told where I was going, and that was for reasons to do with the film rather than any personal wish of my own. It was simply a case of his needing my address.

Dixie hugged me, and stepping back smiled at me briefly through a cloud of silvery hair. Something flicked behind her eyes, something almost like guilt. And then she turned away, wafting clouds of expensive perfume—it was made for her in an exclusive little shop in Collins Street.

'Well, this is certainly different! Are you on a retreat or something, Kate darling?'

I smiled. '"Or something" just about covers it. Where are you staying?'

Dixie began to describe minutely the house someone had lent them. Cecil had come up behind his wife, and caught my eyes over her head, his own full of weary amusement. We all walked around to the front of the cottage.

Dixie pulled a face. 'You really have gone bush, haven't you?'

Suddenly I felt defensive. The cottage may have been old and small, but I held an affection for it that was very powerful. And the view of the river may have been unexciting to one who preferred cityscapes, but to me it had an ever changing beauty and a serenity that was a balm to my soul.

I said as much.

Dixie didn't answer, but gave Cecil a glance with raised eyebrows. 'Did you bring my cigarettes, darling?' she asked him sweetly.

'They're in the car, my love,' Cecil replied with equal sweetness.

Dixie sighed, and trotted off to get them. It was all pretence, I knew that. The Dixie image.

Cecil had sat down on the chair. Looking up, he asked me bluntly, 'Are you all right?'

I thought I was going to say 'yes', but his expression of genuine concern changed my mind. 'No,' I said quietly.

He looked down at his shoes. 'Is it bad?'

'I'm not dying, if that's what you mean. I just need some time alone. The film, you know, and Ian and ... well,' I waved my arm vaguely. 'I need to recharge some batteries. Make some decisions.'

Cecil sighed. 'It was just so unlike you, going off to the bush like that.'

Was it? I asked myself. Or rather, was it unlike Ian? I was beginning to realise at last that Ian and I were two very different people, with different thoughts and wants and wishes. Ian was—or had been—the stronger, always. His character had overwhelmed mine and it was only now that he was gone that I was beginning to rediscover it.

'Dixie was worried,' Cecil said, interrupting my thoughts.

I looked up, surprised.

'She's very fond of you, Kate. She admires you tremendously. And—' But he stopped abruptly, biting his lip.

'Here we are!' Dixie was back, waving her cigarettes, as if nothing could have begun properly without them. 'I couldn't believe it when Jack told me you were here,' she went on, lighting one with a flourish. 'You never said,' with a sharp, sideways glance. 'You never told anyone that you were going off on your own. And here, of all places! Kate, what are you up to?'

'I'm not up to anything,' I retorted, and then managed to soften it with a smile. 'I just wanted some peace and quiet.'

'Which we've managed to destroy,' Cecil murmured.

But Dixie ignored him. 'Surely you could find "peace and quiet" somewhere a bit more interesting than this, Kate! Honestly, the place is falling down!' And she flicked an unflattering glance over the cottage.

'Now, Dixie, it's not for us to choose Kate's holidays for her. If she wants to spend some time alone by the river ...'

Dixie looked hurt. 'I thought she'd be glad to see us!'

I was touched. Dixie meant it, I knew. She was a selfish woman in many ways, but I was fond of her, and during *The Lost Ones* we had had some good times.

Now, remembering those times, I said impulsively, 'Come inside. I'll make you some coffee.'

As soon as we were inside, I regretted it. Dixie laughed at the odd furnishings and exclaimed in horror at the kitchen, much as I had done myself when I first arrived.

'My God, Kate! It's like something out of Henry Lawson ... *The Drover's Wife*!'

Cecil frowned thoughtfully at the stove. 'Nooo, I think *For the Term of His Natural Life*, covers it more aptly, my love.'

I managed to steer the conversation around to business, and Dixie was soon in full flight. 'Jack is talking about a July release for the US. Will you go, Kate? He wants to get as many of the main stars over there as possible. Too late for the Oscars, unfortunately.' She laughed to show that, really, she was joking.

'This year, anyway,' Cecil said.

Dixie ignored him. 'Will you be able to make it, Kate? It won't be the same without you.'

I blinked. 'To the Oscars?'

'No,' with an uneasy glance. 'America in July!'

I stirred my coffee. Ian's voice was screaming in my head. If he had been here, he would have jumped at America. In fact, he probably would have thought of it before Jack did. He'd have had a schedule packed full of engagements for me to attend, interviews to give and people to meet. *This is it*, he'd have said. *This is your chance for Hollywood.*

'Oh Kate,' Dixie wailed, 'you must come!'

I heard my own voice, strangely calm. 'I'll have to see.'

'Dixie,' Cecil said it sharply, for him. 'Leave the girl alone. Kate must make up her own mind. Not everyone enjoys jaunting all over the place, talking about themselves, like you do.'

I glanced at him sideways, wondering just how much Cecil suffered for Dixie's ambition.

Dixie was glaring at him. 'Kate is *supposed* to be the star. Jack wants her to go. If Ian was here, he'd make her go. Just because she's got the Greta Garbos doesn't mean she can bail out and leave all the hard work to the rest of us. Work's the best thing, Cecil, you know that! Ian knew that!'

I wondered why they were talking about me as if I wasn't there. I sensed an undercurrent that had nothing to do with the conversation they were having. What on earth was wrong with them?

They had stopped, and were waiting for me to answer, both watching to see which I would favour.

'I'm not bailing out,' I explained quietly. 'And I haven't said I won't go. 'I'm "resting" in the truest sense of the word.'

Dixie opened her mouth, and the phone rang. From inside her purse.

Cecil rolled his eyes. 'I thought we agreed to leave that thing at home.'

'How could I? It might be important.'

'Well, take it outside then, so we don't have to listen.'

Dixie glared at him, but went. We could hear her on the verandah, speaking in loud, cheerful tones. I glanced at Cecil and forced a smile. 'She's right, you know. It might be important. An actor can't afford not to be available.'

'Yes, it might be Kenneth Branagh!' but he smiled back.

Suddenly afraid he would begin questioning me again, I said, 'This place is supposed to be haunted, you know.'

Cecil leaned forward. 'You do surprise me.'

I grinned. 'No, really.'

'Have you seen the ghost then?' He was only half joking.

'I've seen ... something.'

He looked into my face. 'I don't think this is the right place for you, Kate,' he said quietly.

'No, really, joking aside. It's ... creepy. I felt it as
we drove in. Come back to Hobart with us. You
don't have to stay at our house, you can find
somewhere on your own,' he added quickly,
reading my thoughts.

For a moment I was tempted. If I went, I
wouldn't have to see Devlin again, or listen to
that boat coming towards me across the river. I
could pack my things now and be out of here in
less than an hour. I could be on a plane to Melbourne, and home by dark. And then?

Beyond the cottage, the river swirled and
rippled, while Dixie's voice droned on. What was
there for me at home? Bolten and his further
tests, the brittle, artificial life of Kate O'Hara,
the actor. Suddenly I knew I didn't want to leave
the cottage. This place had insinuated itself into
my heart and soul. The past had begun to matter
to me more than the present, and certainly more
than the future.

'No,' I said at last. 'Thank you, Cecil, but no.'
'You must miss Ian.'
I looked at him in surprise. 'Yes, of course.'
Cecil shifted his position in the chair. 'Did
you know ... ' he broke off, and began again. 'Ian
never told you, did he?' There was something in
his eyes, the sort of pain I recognised well.

I felt my face go numb. 'I knew he was
unfaithful,' I whispered. 'I knew about his little
affairs. But he would never have left me. He
swore he would never leave me. He was always
there when I needed him, always!'

My voice had risen, as if I were trying to convince myself that that was all that mattered. Cecil put out a hand and then let it drop. He looked miserable, and old. My anger evaporated. 'Not Dixie?' I whispered. 'Not her, too?'

'One thing about Ian, he believed in equality,' Cecil joked weakly. 'Everyone got their share.'

'Oh Cecil …' I felt saddened and ashamed.

He shrugged. 'Dixie thought she had met her "soulmate",' he said with a savage mockery I had not heard from him before. 'But Ian was only after a couple of days' intensive screwing. After that, he was quite happy to move on. And he was never going to leave you, Kate. You were the goose that laid the golden eggs, weren't you? Or did he love you, do you think, in some strange, cerebral, Ian way?'

His bitterness stung me but I understood it. I understood it all too well. Ian, the strong man who had taken over my life and career and pushed me into fame, had also been a weak man when it came to sexual temptation. That was what the argument in the car had been about, the night of the accident. I had caught Ian out, again, in one of his sordid lies, and suddenly I couldn't bear it any more. I couldn't accept that he loved me and yet could still betray me with such effortless regularity.

I don't keep you on a leash, do I? His voice whispered in my ear. He had said that in the car, his eyes hot with anger. And he hadn't kept me on a leash. I had had my share of lovers, just to show Ian I could, and a couple of them even ended up as friends. But, mostly, my career ruled me, Ian saw to that, and there was little time for thoughts of anything else. Sometimes, in my rare moments alone, I had allowed myself to consider the future, and I had known, with a frightened sense of being caged, that this wasn't what I wanted from my life. This wasn't the reason I had married Ian. I couldn't, no matter how I tried, understand his unfaithfulness and his total unwillingness, or perhaps inability, to change.

It must be, I had thought, that he did not love me enough, or that I wasn't the sort of woman who could transform him into a doting, faithful husband. My longing to be that woman explained my compliance as he gradually took over my life, and remade me as 'Kate O'Hara, actor'. And now it was all over, and I was glad!

'It doesn't matter,' Cecil was saying. 'Kate? Kate, really, it doesn't matter. He's dead now, anyway, isn't he.'

'Yes,' I whispered. 'Yes, he's dead now.'

Dixie's steps tapped quickly down the passage towards us. 'Cecil!' She could hardly wait until she was in the kitchen to begin speaking. 'That was Elaine. She's been talking with George and there's the chance of a part in his next movie!' She was gathering her things together, and Cecil was climbing reluctantly to his feet.

'So we're leaving? We only just got here, Dixie!'

'I'm sorry, but we must.' A faint, deprecatory smile for me. '*You* understand, Kate, don't you? Elaine is sending a script for me to look at, and she'll try and get George to ring me at the house. I can't *not* be there, can I?'

'I understand!' I said, and I did. This was Dixie's life, and it had been my life until very recently. But it was my life no longer, and I did not feel even a little bit sad to see it go. I felt almost sorry for Dixie and Cecil.

Cecil gave me a hasty kiss, murmured, 'Forget what I said! Ring us as soon as you get home!' and went to start the car.

Dixie looked at me, her eyes full of guilt. I realised then that it had been the guilt, not friendship, which brought her here, seeking me out. This was some sort of cathartic exercise for her ... for them both. Poor Dixie, I understood only too well how Ian could be when he wanted something. So persuasive, so charming. And then when he didn't want it any more he could be such a bastard. Should I hate Dixie for what had happened? Should I hate Ian? I had gone past hate. I had a new life to build.

Dixie gave me a determined smile, and suddenly I admired her for her guts. 'Enjoy your holiday, Kate darling. Oh!' she turned back. 'That man in the boat on the river ... he rowed across while I was talking with Elaine on the phone. Rather a hunk, isn't he? Love the pony-tail! I think I can understand why you're here, after all!'

She didn't give me time to answer. She was already gone, her perfume floating after her.

I turned sharply, facing the river. The water lay still and empty. My mind seemed to be tumbling over and over, like an acrobat at a circus.

'Devlin?' I whispered.

But the silence was my only answer.

6

I couldn't settle after Dixie and Cecil had gone. Their presence lingered in the cottage with Dixie's stale cigarette smoke, and memories of Ian.

Their visit had merely reinforced my certainty that I had left their life forever.

I stood up, restlessly, and looked out of the window. It was early, and yet half of me was already wishing the day at an end ... while the other half wanted the darkness never to come.

I went to take out my paints, and then

changed my mind and picked up Howard Tuck's book instead. Amazing, I thought wryly, how so thin a book could be such an arduous task to read. Sitting down on the sofa, with the sun warming my shoulders, I inspected it.

Howard appeared on the back cover. An old photo, so old it was almost a painting. He looked short and fat and pompous, just as I would have expected. I opened the book at the end papers, wondering if it had an index, and berating myself for not looking before.

There was no index, but there was a map.

With growing excitement, I realised it was a hand drawn map of the Leeward area, including the river and the site of the old convict barracks. The cottage appeared as a square box with the words 'Private Property' marked on it.

The barracks were shown as three rectangles surrounding a courtyard, upriver from the cottage, and nearby was an area denoted 'quarry'. A walking track led in from the highway, and I tried to work out just how far the barracks would be overland from the cottage. Not far on the map, but perhaps it wasn't drawn to scale—there were no measurements on it.

It might be interesting to take a look. Let's face it, I wasn't doing much else, was I? I fetched my purse and keys, and went out to the car.

I grinned to myself as I followed the rough road back to the highway. No wonder Dixie had been so appalled! The smile faded. Dixie and Ian. I should have realised. They were so alike, they would naturally be drawn together. I had read somewhere once that human beings were composed of dark and light, opposing forces. Sometimes the dark or evil in them triumphed and sometimes the light or good did. It was a simplistic view, but it fitted Ian perfectly. It was as if he were two men in one, the good and the bad, and neither would meld with the other.

There weren't many other cars on the highway. A couple of timber trucks roared past me, and I made as much room for them as I could. The blast of diesel and sawn logs took my breath away, and I'd hardly recovered from the experience when I saw the small rustic-looking sign on the other side of the road.

'Walking Track—Historic Site.'

With a quick glance behind me to check if there were any more timber trucks about to bear down on me, I swung across the road and pulled up off the bitumen into the curved bay provided.

The track looked well kept, a clear way through the bush. I locked up the car and, tying the sweater I had brought with me around my waist, set off. After only a few steps I came upon another sign, with an arrow, stating: 'Historic Site—3 kms, easy walking.'

Easy walking, I thought. It sounded made for me. Striding out, I set off again in the direction of the arrow.

Behind me, the sound of cars and trucks quickly faded. The silence was broken only by the songs of birds and the small crackles of the bush and my own passage through it. The scent of the trees cleared my senses and I felt my skin begin to tingle from the exercise and the fresh air. *This* is what I came here for, I told myself. This feeling of confidence and well-being. Who needed Hollywood?

So you'd throw it all away, would you? Ian's voice mocked me softly. *All my hard work.*

'*Your* hard work?' I muttered. '*I* was there, too, remember?'

But Ian was sulking, and didn't answer.

The three kilometres were quickly covered. I came to a large cleared area, which was showing signs of being reclaimed by the bush. There seemed to be nothing there but a timber-framed board, placed by some efficient government department to inform tourists of the significance of the site. As I drew closer, I could see that there was a printed sheet, under glass, giving a brief history of the Leeward area, and informing me that this was the site of the convict barracks, burned down in July 1829.

'Ten convicts escaped, but were subsequently recaptured without further incident. The fire, whether deliberately lit or not, burned the barrack buildings to the ground.'

The notice went on to say that the area had been excavated and several interesting pieces found, including chains, a soldier's boot, pieces of crockery and horse shoes.

'Fascinating,' I murmured dryly.

I glanced about and caught a glimpse of the

river through the trees. I was close to it, then. Somehow, that was a comforting thought. Slowly, I strolled about the cleared space, trying to make out where the barracks had been, but it was just about impossible. There were no neat rectangles here, as there had been on the map, and probably souvenir hunters and local home-builders had reclaimed any bricks or stone or timber which were lying about after the fire. It seemed hardly worth the effort of putting up the board and keeping the area clear.

A chill breeze puffed across the clearing. I shivered and reached to undo my sweater from around my waist, pulling it on. As the soft, fleecy cloth slipped down over my face, something caught my attention.

The white cat.

It was sitting on the ground near the edge of the bush, watching me.

For a split second, I thought it was a different animal. But as I examined it more carefully, I realised it was indeed the cat from the cottage. I could not mistake that glowing white fur and those yellow eyes. Perhaps the cat lived here. The cottage couldn't be far across country, through the bush, and a cat would know the most direct ways. For all I knew, the thing might roam for dozens of square kilometres along the river!

The cat hadn't moved, its stillness almost intimidating. When the breeze stirred its fur, I felt a sense of relief. I had begun to think it must be a ghost, like Devlin. Tentatively, I took a step towards it. The animal seemed to shrink slightly with tension, its yellow eyes fixed unwaveringly on my progress. Slowly, walking with exaggerated care, I inched towards it.

'Puss, Puss?'

The cat straightened and then leaned forward, stretching onto its front paws and arching its back. It gave itself a shake, and began to pad towards me, tail held aloft like a flag.

I smiled and gently flicked my fingers towards it. 'Here puss, good puss.'

The cat padded on, confident, its yellow eyes fixed on mine. I waited, eager to make this first contact. It looked more like someone's pet than the wild cats I was used to seeing in Melbourne back streets, with their matted coats and ragged ears.

The cat reached me and ignoring my fingers, it brushed instead against my bare leg. I was smiling; this was an important victory for me.

And then the clearing turned into chaos.

The sky was black, night black, and flames crackled and burning debris spun in the air and smoke belched. The screams of horses pierced the shouts and thuds of running men. I was standing close to a burning building ... too close. One of the timbers fell with a whoosh of embers and I flinched, terrified, as the gust of hot air passed over me.

CHAPTER SIX

I knew I should turn and run, run as fast and as far as I could. But my mind was numb with shock and disbelief. Someone grabbed roughly at my arm with bruising fingers, pulling me back to safety. Now I was standing beside what looked like a small hut. Through the open door, in the bright light of the fire, I glimpsed crates and barrels and sacks. Another crash of falling timber, and I stumbled, shading my eyes from the brilliance of the flames. I seemed to be alone here by the hut, and I looked around wildly to see if anyone else was nearby.

'What are you doing here?'

I wasn't alone after all. The man who had pulled me to safety was glaring at me through reddened eyes. His face was smeared with black soot and running with sweat, his fair hair was flattened by the heat and festooned with flakes of ash. His white shirt was streaked with black, too, and his trousers were torn at the knee. He had some sort of sword buckled to his side. He's a soldier, I thought in amazement.

'I asked you what you are doing here,' he repeated firmly.

'I'm on holiday,' I said, knowing for sure now that I was going mad.

He gave me a look that seemed to agree, and walked away, shouting so loudly I jumped. 'Get that water over here! Now, you whoreson!'

Whoreson? I asked myself. *Whoreson?*

Another soldier was running with a couple of horses, trying to control their struggling and lead them to safety. One shrieked, pawing the air with sharp hooves, but the soldier heaved it savagely down, his mouth open in a steady stream of curses, most of them, like 'whoreson', foreign to me.

My numbness was beginning to thaw, and I stared around me, not knowing what to think. God, this was better than any movie! What would Bolten have to say about this? Were hallucinations always this lifelike, or were mine special? The small clearing seemed to have grown into the size of a football ground. Carts were jumbled at one end with the horses, and everywhere men ran, faces like devils in the firelight, or sat, coughing up smoke. The barracks building itself was much larger than I had imagined from the map. And it was well alight.

Someone jolted against me, and I turned and looked into a grim, lined face. He wore a dirty yellow jacket, blackened in places by the fire— the sort of jacket a convict would wear. His feet were bare, and one of them was bleeding. His skin looked like old leather, and his nose had been broken more than once. The firelight was so bright, I could even see the colour of his eyes, and the expression in them.

It was beyond redemption. A face that had been moulded by cruelty and misery and hatred.

'You'll come with me, Kate,' he said in a thick, smoke-affected voice.

I gaped at him, too amazed to answer.

And then the soldier with the sword was back beside me. 'Get on to the bucket brigade!' he shouted. 'Move, you whoreson!' The educated, British accent and the assumption of leadership all pointed to the fact that this man was Major Dunwich.

The convict hesitated, and then vanished into the smoke. I peered after him nervously. Kate, he had called me. Or had he? Had it been a mistake? Were there two Kates running around here in this hellish madness?

'Put your backs into it!' screamed Dunwich. I stumbled as the bucket brigade surged past me. You won't save it, I felt like saying. The whole lot is going to burn to the ground. You'd better get started rounding up the ten escaped convicts.

Another rafter fell with a crash into the heart of the fire, and the bucket brigade retreated, some holding their hands to their eyes to shield them from the painful brilliant heat.

Just for a second I could see right through the middle of what had been the barracks, to the other side. There was a tall dark shadow there, moving. My breath caught in my throat. Devlin? Was he here, too? The paragraph about him in Howard's book came back to me with sudden clarity. Devlin had helped fight the fire and save lives, he had dragged semiconscious convicts to safety. Devlin was here!

I ran forward, intending to skirt around the fire and make my way to the other side. 'Devlin!' I cried. 'Is it you, Devlin?'

'Get back. It's not safe.' Major Dunwich stepped in front of me, effectively blocking my way. I banged into him and came to an abrupt halt. He smelt of smoke and sweat, and his stomach was of a soft, flabby consistency. He gripped my arm, but he was looking over at the barracks, where flames were leaping high into the night sky. It appeared that they were no longer trying to save it. 'What a waste,' he snorted. 'Someone will have to pay for this, eh, Cromarty?'

I thought he was still addressing me, and I gazed, like some fire-dazed creature, up at his profile. It was straight and rather aristocratic. And then the smoke cleared and, as if by magic, there appeared a man with the roundest face I had ever seen, and the piggiest eyes. 'Aye, sir,' he said in a greasy, obsequious voice. 'We'll have the truth out of 'em all right, sir.'

Cromarty? I thought. This couldn't be Cromarty, the dreaded overseer, who flogged his prisoners once a day and twice on Sundays. This was more like John Candy on a bad day.

'The governor will want a detailed report,' Dunwich went on. 'He's most particular when it comes to detail. It wouldn't surprise me if he inspects the damage himself.'

Cromarty nodded, his piggy eyes veiled.

'I want you to see to it, Cromarty.'

'Aye, I will sir, don't you worry none, sir, it'll be dealt with, sir.'

I couldn't believe Dunwich would take the man seriously, but evidently he was used to such grovelling. He now turned his attention to me, and seemed to be having trouble coming to terms with my skirt and sweater.

'What are you doing here?' he repeated the question he had asked earlier. 'You were calling for Devlin. Are you this Devlin's wife?'

I opened my mouth, but it was Cromarty who answered.

'Devlin ain't got a wife, Major. This is his woman, sir.'

His woman? I turned and stared at him. He was smirking at me.

'She's been livin' over at his cottage, sir.'

Major Dunwich let his eyes slide over me in a way that made me long to shrink inside my clothing. 'Indeed,' he said. 'What is your name, madam?'

I began to feel edgy. If I were him, I would be looking for scapegoats, and a lone, strange woman probably fitted the bill perfectly.

'I'm just visiting,' I muttered, and shuffled back. Cromarty grabbed my arm, but as he moved one of the soldiers came running. 'They're out, sir!' he was shouting. 'They've bolted!'

Major Dunwich and his henchman lost interest in me.

'How many?' he boomed.

'About a dozen, sir,' the man replied breathlessly. He had a nasty gash on his cheek.

'Check on the weapons!' Dunwich shouted—he couldn't seem to give any order without shouting it. The three men ran towards the other side of the clearing, vanishing into the clouds of sparks and smoke.

I breathed a sigh of relief. But I knew Dunwich would be back; he had the look of a man who disliked unfinished business. I began to shuffle even further into the shadowy trees before they remembered me again. The air was heavy with burning, overpowering the sweeter smells of earth and leaf mould. My throat felt raw. So many things had happened in such a short space of time. I couldn't begin to digest them. I put my hand up to a branch, and felt its roughness beneath my fingers. The bark gave off a faint peppermint scent. I moved closer, to rest my face against it, and stopped, frozen.

There was something behind me.

My flesh tingled with apprehension. I expected any moment to feel hands grip me. Something rustled near my foot, and I made a sound, low in my throat, half-groan and half-whimper. There was a soft, furry sensation against my ankle and then my head began to spin. I sank down onto the ground as the sounds about me slowly faded into silence.

Sunlight flickered through the leaves and a bird began to sing. I lifted my head and found that I was sitting in the clearing, quite alone. The white cat rushed past me, low to the ground, and vanished into the bush. Everything was exactly the same as it had been before.

Once back at the cottage, I knew I should call Bolten. I knew it, but could not bring myself to do it. What had happened to me in the clearing had been so real, so vivid ... and yet such things did not happen. There were scientific laws governing them ... weren't there? Travelling through time was a subject for fiction, not fact. It must have been a hallucination!

But that didn't explain the smell of smoke that saturated my hair and clothing, and the five dark bruises on my upper arm, where someone had grabbed me too tightly, and all I had seen and heard and experienced.

You're going stark staring mad, Ian's voice sounded in my head.

'If I am, it's your fault!' I shouted back.

I put my head in my hands and tried to think logically, to balance the events of the past few days which had really happened against those I could have hallucinated. Devlin's boat on the river? Well, that could have been any old fisherman. Devlin's appearances? Someone had mentioned ghosts to me, and my mind took over, creating one suitable for the part. The scene at the clearing? That could have been half Howard and half guess. The characters? Well, they were reasonably standard: Dunwich, the stern, English officer; Cromarty, the sly, grovelling overseer; and the oppressed convicts. The smell of smoke on me? The wood fire in the kitchen could explain that. And the bruises? I had heard of cases of bruises just appearing on a person's arm, and even stigmata! The power of the mind was very strong.

All I had seen and heard could be explained by the hallucination theory ... just. That left Dixie. Dixie had seen a man in a boat on the river, and Dixie was no hysteric. Of course, she may have simply seen a fisherman. And yet, I had seen nothing only moments afterwards. Could a fisherman have rowed on and vanished so quickly?

The doubt was enough to raise my spirits.

I longed to believe that I had stumbled upon something wondrous, something beyond most people's comprehension, something I must pursue to a conclusion. I had seen people long dead, I had walked among them—Major Dunwich, Cromarty and Devlin. Briefly, the empty eyes of the convict in the dirty jacket flashed into my mind. 'You'll come with me, Kate,' he had said. I shivered.

Automatically, I set about preparing my evening meal, not because I was hungry but because it would be night soon, and I needed something to do. I wasn't ready to face Devlin again, not yet. So after I had eaten and climbed into bed, I reached for Bolten's sleeping tablets. And lay drowsily, watching the candle dance in the draught from the window as my thoughts floated and faded into darkness.

I tried to wake, my eyelids too heavy to open. It was very late and very still. Sleep was pulling at me, dragging me down. There was a sense of someone being in the room with me. A voice murmured my name, the sound far away and yet close by. And then it was gone.

It was blustery the next day, bending the trees and making the surface of the river choppy. I drove into Leeward. It was necessary to replenish my supplies, or I probably would not have gone. But without a fridge, I was limited in what I could buy and keep fresh.

As I was placing the grocery bags in the car, I thought of the museum and old Jim Wallace. If there was anyone who might have information on the fire, it was him. If it meant I could convince myself of my sanity, I was willing to grasp at straws.

I made my way towards the museum, battling to hold my hair out of my eyes as the wind tried to blow it into them. The stuffed animals greeted me silently, and I wandered through the rooms, listening to the echo of my footsteps. The photograph of the cottage was in the same place, and I bent to look at it.

'What do you want, Devlin?' I whispered. 'Where did you go?'

'Kate, you're back again!'

Startled, and hoping he hadn't heard me, I turned around. Jim Wallace seemed glad to see me. His pale eyes were twinkling.

'How are you getting on with Howard Tuck's book?'

I smiled back. 'I'm about halfway through. I've read the bit about the fire ... or most of it. I was wondering ... do you have any pictures of what the convict barracks looked like? I imagine it would be too early for photos?'

He tapped his cheek with a finger. 'Yes. There are some original drawings in Hobart, and we have copies in storage here. If you'd like to wait, I'll have a quick look for you.' His mouth curled up at the corner, 'As you can see, Kate, I'm run off my feet.'

I laughed. He felt like an old friend.

While I waited, I spent some time at a display of old farming implements. Amazing the work they used to do with a horse and a stump-jump plough!

'Not much, I'm afraid.' Jim Wallace was back, with a folder of papers in his hands. 'As you can see, the barracks were built of timber, pretty rough and ready, I'd say. There were cells for the prisoners—they were all locked in at night—and quarters for the soldiers, probably one big room. The overseer had a room to himself. Then there'd be a cook room and wash room, all very primitive. They didn't believe in rehabilitating prisoners in those days, just punishing them.'

'So I've heard.'

The drawing was of a large building, three sides around a courtyard, as it had appeared on the map in the back of Howard's book. It looked near enough to what I had seen, or what was left of it, burning in the clearing.

'I have these, too,' Jim went on, shuffling his papers. They were photocopies, a couple with photographs attached. 'They excavated the site of the fire, you know, and found some interesting things.'

I looked at a photograph of a horseshoe and tried not to cross my eyes with boredom. The last photocopy snapped me out of it. 'What's that?'

Jim frowned, trying to read the heading upside down. 'That was part of a notebook. It belonged to one of the founders of this museum, but was supposed to have originally come from someone at the barracks. I don't know if that's the truth or legend. Anyway, it's old. Amazing to have lasted so long. You see the writing?'

I bent closer to see, but couldn't read it. The author must have been a spider, I thought, weaving all over the page, and the dark spots of damp and mould did not help.

'It's written in blood,' Jim Wallace said quietly.

I looked up at him. 'Blood?' I gasped.

'He probably didn't have access to ink.' I looked at the photocopy again, this time with a sense of fascinated revulsion. 'Do you know what it says? I'm afraid I can't read it.'

'There's a transcript here ...' He shuffled again, and brought out a small piece of paper which he handed to me with some ceremony. He had my attention now, and he knew it.

I began to read the typed sheet. It was a rambling diatribe on hell and the devil. And it was disturbing, if only because the person who wrote it obviously believed what he was saying. According to him, man was a basically evil creature who must be punished for the saving of his soul. And woman! Well, woman was something you scraped off your boot!

'The bitch grins and lies, and the maggot turns in her soul. Burn it out with the pure fire.'

101

I read, pulling a face and handing it back to Jim. 'Not the sort of person I'd want to have a meaningful conversation with. Do they know whose it was?'

'Unfortunately, no. The language is that of an educated man—if you discount the content—and the spelling is pretty good for a time when words were more or less spelt phonetically. It seems unlikely many of the convicts could write, so unless it was one of the few more literate ones, it probably belonged to the overseer Cromarty or one of the soldiers.'

'I'd go for Cromarty,' I murmured. 'It sounds like his sort of thing.'

Jim looked at me strangely. 'You know a bit about Cromarty, Kate?'

'No ... I, well, just what I read in Howard Tuck's book.'

'Ah, I see.'

It was time to change the subject. 'Did anyone ever find out what happened to Devlin, the boatman?' I asked quietly.

'There's no trace of him after the fire. No burial records or official records of his death, and nothing in any of the convict records—other than the original one, of course.'

Something inside me lifted its head, like a hound on a scent. 'Original one?'

'Yes, he was originally sent out to Van Diemen's Land as a convict. I'm sorry, didn't I mention that before?' He smiled faintly, 'Sometimes I don't. People aren't as touchy about these things as they used to be, but some are still quite upset when they find a convict in their cupboard. Though from a genealogical point of view, the convict records are very detailed. You can find out the colour of your ancestor's eyes and hair, how tall he was, what he did for a living, where he came from —a great wealth of information.'

'What did Devlin do wrong?' I was holding my breath, and forced it slowly out. What did it matter? I asked myself crossly. Devlin was a hallucination. But somehow it did matter, it mattered very much.

'Rebellion, I believe,' Jim replied, with that glimmer in his eye telling me he knew he had my total attention. 'Fourteen years' transportation, but he had his ticket-of-leave in six, and a conditional pardon soon after. That meant he could live as a free man in the colony, under the condition he never returned home to Ireland.'

'So he wasn't really free,' I said.

'No, I suppose he wasn't.'

'I wonder where he disappeared to, and why.'

Jim Wallace shook his head. 'I don't know, Kate. No-one knows. Perhaps you'll find out for us, eh?'

Perhaps I will, I thought. Perhaps I'll ask him next time he comes to see me.

The weather hadn't improved when I left the museum. The leaves were blowing around the streets and falling from the trees like golden rain. I hunched into my sweater and kept my head down. I was past Linda Kearns's craft shop when I heard her calling me, and turned back. She was standing in the doorway, and her comfortable smile was like summer sunlight. The breeze was blowing into her shop, tugging at the windchimes hanging from the ceiling and making them sing, while the dreamcatchers danced to the tune, light as air.

'My son finished your painting,' she said, before I could ask. 'I told him you weren't in a hurry, but he had nothing else to do.'

I followed Linda into the shop, and watched as she lifted the painting out from under the counter, laying it onto the flat surface for my inspection.

The transformation was amazing.

What before had been dark and gloomy now seemed soft and muted. The artist had set his scene at night, but with plenty of moonlight to illuminate it. The cottage stood still and dark above the riverbank, and yet one felt it was awake and watchful. The river flowed in silver ripples. But I didn't look closely at any of that.

The boatman was rowing on the river. He was facing the artist, shoulders bent as he drew the oars through the water, dark head bowed, so that his face was partly shadowed. My heart began to thump. It was easy, too easy, to transpose upon that half-seen face the face of the ghost who had stood in my doorway.

But the boatman wasn't alone. There was another person in the boat. A woman with pale hair—blonde or white, it was hard to tell—with her back turned to the artist. She was leaning back, taking her ease, with her hand trailing in the silver water.

'My son says there's a story about the river,' Linda said softly, as I gazed spellbound at the picture. 'It's supposed to be haunted by a man who rows his boat back and forth. Sometimes he's alone, and sometimes he has someone with him.'

I nodded slowly.

'He's done a good job of cleaning it up, hasn't he?' She was justly proud of her son's effort.

'Yes. Yes, he has.' I tried to snap myself out of it, but I couldn't seem to take my eyes off the boatman's face. 'Thank him for me.'

I paid the bill, a ridiculously small amount for the miracle he had wrought. Linda wrapped the painting carefully, chatting, and then handed me the awkward parcel.

'My son was out on your stretch of the river yesterday,' she went on with a smile. 'He says you had visitors. I hope he wasn't disturbing you? He enjoys getting out in the boat when he's home.'

I stared. 'Your son?' I repeated blankly. 'He was on the river yesterday morning?'

'Yes.' Linda kept smiling, but something about my reaction brought a puzzled look to her eyes.

'I ... does he have dark hair?'

Linda nodded, her smile turning into a grimace. 'And one of those ponytails, I'm afraid.'

'How old is your son?' I asked quietly.

'Nineteen. He's studying art at uni. The restoration work brings in a bit of pocket money for him. He hopes to find a job in one of the galleries or museums, doing the same sort of thing.'

'Wish him luck for me,' I said, wondering how I could sound so calm when I was reeling.

Nineteen was too young for Devlin, and too young for me. But if Dixie had seen only the back of his head ... and how did I know what Dixie considered too young! She had seen a man, and assumed he was my latest, and I had assumed ... well, I had assumed she had seen Devlin.

The painting was very heavy under my arm as I carried it back to the car. It had been Linda Kearns's young son whom Dixie had seen on the river, not Devlin's ghost. How could I have ever thought otherwise? Devlin did not exist. I was hallucinating, or going mad. I should ring Bolten now—immediately.

I told you so, Ian mocked.

I was too devastated even to answer him. Although I hadn't admitted it to myself, Dixie's sighting of my 'ghost' had been one of my major points against having hallucinated the whole thing. Dixie, I had decided, had seen Devlin, therefore Devlin was 'real'. Except that Dixie had actually seen Linda Kearns's son.

The pay phone was outside the general store. A woman burdened with a pram and a toddler was using it, trying to concentrate on what the person on the other end was saying while rocking the pram with her foot and holding the toddler with a firm hand.

I waited.

Their conversation seemed endless. The baby in the pram began to scream, and the toddler joined in, struggling wildly in its mother's grip. Against such odds the mother could not win. She hung up and marched off, dragging her child with her.

I slipped the coins into the slot and dialled the number. My fingers were shaking. I felt as if my heart were in my throat like a great lump, preventing me from speaking.

'Dr Bolten's office.' The voice was brisk but friendly.

'Hello, Karen? This is Kate O'Hara. I wondered if I could speak to your boss.'

Karen's voice became even warmer than before. 'Ms O'Hara! Yes, of course you can speak to him. The thing is, he's off this morning. I can get him for you at home, if you like, or he can call you back after lunch.'

Against all good sense, I felt I had been reprieved. Relief caused me to slump against the glass side of the telephone box, as if all the bones in my body had melted. My voice came from somewhere, oddly untouched. 'I ... no, look, I'll call him back. I don't have a phone at the cottage, so I have to come into town and use the public one.'

'Oh.' Karen didn't sound happy about that.

'I'll call back this afternoon or ... or tomorrow,' I added in a rush.

'OK.' But she drew the word out, not quite approving. 'Can you tell me what the problem is, and perhaps I can give Dr Bolten a call and he can decide whether he needs to talk with you now or—'.

'Oh no,' I burst out, 'it's nothing serious. Just a question or two. I'll ring back, Karen. Thanks for your help.'

And I hung up.

The silence was blissful. I felt ashamed. Bolten was a nice man, a caring man, but I was afraid of what he would say and do. I did not want to leave the cottage, not yet. Hallucination or not, I did not want to leave Devlin.

It gave me a great sense of pleasure to hang the painting back over the mantelpiece. It shone gently, now, rather than glowering darkly. I gazed up at the boatman's secretive face. Was that the gleam of an eye? Was he looking back at me? If I stared long enough, I would begin to believe it.

Linda Kearns's son had replaced the heavy old frame with a lighter timber one. I could see the title, *The Boatman*, without any trouble. But no artist. If I had been hoping for more revelations, I was to be disappointed.

After lunch, I read some more of Howard's book. He had moved to some southern port and a career with a shipbuilding uncle. He dabbled in politics for a while, and married late in life a young widow with several children. He died in 1911, aged ninety years.

I set the book aside, feeling strangely sad and let down. 'Well, that's that,' I told myself.

Outside, the afternoon was merging into evening. The wind cut at the river, chopping it into little white-crested waves. I turned and looked up at the painting above the mantelpiece. There was an ache inside me I could not explain.

You're pining for a dead man? Ian asked, bewildered and cross. *Devlin's even deader than me! Whatever happened to him after the fire in 1829, he'd have to be dead by now.*

'Yes.'

Focus, Kate, for God's sake!

I stood up, not wanting to listen. I didn't want to focus. I wanted to dream and drift. I wanted to let myself float, like mad Ophelia in the river. I wanted to believe the unbelievable.

I turned my back on the painting and stared out of the window at the wild scene. The cat was sitting by the old jetty, huddled in the grass, the wind playing games with its fur. As I watched, a squall of rain came across the river, churning up the surface even more and obscuring my view for a few seconds until it passed over. When I could see again, the cat had gone.

8

I woke late, my mind befuddled by sleeping tablets. This time I remembered nothing of the night. I had taken the medication at eight o'clock, wishing to block out the sound of the wind and rain as much as anything else that might happen. I had slept like the dead for twelve hours, and when I woke I felt groggy and had a nasty taste in my mouth.

The weather had improved. The wind had blown itself out, leaving one of those still, golden autumn days. After lunch, I shook off my inertia, changed into shorts and a T-shirt, and carried my paints out onto the verandah. The river glowed softly and I saw a fish jump. The act of painting took me over, and I soon lost myself in it, forgetting everything else. The tranquillity of the place reached out and enfolded me, soothing my jangled nerves and frightened thoughts. My breathing slowed to the rhythm of the water.

I didn't notice the sun swing around, the shadows lengthening and the air growing chilly and damp. It was only when at last I finished and looked up that I realised it was growing late. I was cold. But I was happy with the result.

I stretched my arms above my head, smiling to myself. Across the water, as if on cue, the evening bird circled and found a place to land. It floated, oblivious to me, settling its feathers. Everything was very still. If I stared long enough, I knew I would begin to imagine a boat gliding over the river towards me.

I shivered and started to gather up my things, bending to pick up my shoes. The cat was sitting behind me, on the very edge of the verandah. It was watching me, its white fur a pale fuzzy blur in the approaching darkness.

I stared at it as if it were a Bengal tiger.

It didn't move. Suddenly it occurred to me that the cat had been there, at the site of the barracks, just before I had found myself back at the time of the fire, and it had been there, still, when I returned. Perhaps—I groped my way towards a conclusion—perhaps the cat had something to do with all this?

Sure, a time-hopping cat, Ian mocked.

I smiled. It was ridiculous. And yet, it was a possibility, and there was only one way to test it out, wasn't there? Besides, I had nothing to lose.

I began to walk towards the cat, feeling slightly foolish. 'Come here, kitty!' I called quietly. 'Let's have a look at you.'

The cat stared at me, unblinking. It probably thought I was as mad as I thought myself.

'Puss? Puss?' I came to a halt before it, still holding out my hand. The cat ignored it, and began to wash its paw. My fingers were shaking as I moved them closer, closer. I placed my hand gently on the cat's silky head.

The world went black.

'Oh God,' I breathed, 'not again.'

It had been evening, with the sky turning pink and mauve and the light gently fading. Now it was night.

I stood up, unable to believe, almost paralysed with terror. A cold, damp wind blew off the river, chilling me to the bone as I stood there in my shorts and T-shirt. A curlew gave its mournful, warning cry.

I had a glimpse of something white, running, and realised it was the cat spearing down the bank towards the river. I went after it. At the edge of the verandah I leapt off, misjudged ... and fell flat on my face.

Dazed, I lay with the wind knocked out of me, wondering what had happened. I didn't like this, I didn't like this at all! How could I be hallucinating? I couldn't possibly have persuaded my mind into believing the cat would transport me back in time. I hadn't even believed it would really happen! So, did that mean this was real?

Slowly, I lifted my head, half blinded by the fall and the darkness, and looked around me. I could see the shape of the cottage, but it looked different. The roofline seemed wrong, flatter somehow. And there was a glow of light in one of the rooms when I knew very well I had not been inside to light a candle.

I've hit my head and I'm seeing things, I told myself in a calm inner voice that, like a dam, held back the swollen waters of hysteria. In a moment I'll wake up and it'll be all right again.

I squeezed my eyes tightly shut, holding my breath, and then opened them wide. It was still dark, the faint flickering light was still there, and the subtle but obvious differences in the cottage were still evident. I groaned softly to myself, and then behind me I heard the soft lap of the river.

I turned my head sharply, breath rasping in my throat, afraid that I would see Devlin walking towards me. But there was only the empty river and the moon, that had been hidden before by clouds and was now peeping out, sweeping a silver track across the water.

Even as relief swirled through me, I thought it was beautiful. Odd that I could appreciate the beauty of the scene while my heart was pounding like a steam train. Then someone moved about in the cottage behind me. I turned to stare. A shadow passed across the window, a dark shape against the light, and a voice spoke in a soft murmur.

I crouched, not knowing what to do. There was someone in the cottage, and I had a feeling I knew who it was. And if it was who I thought it was, I had to see him. I crawled towards the lighted window.

The bricks that paved the verandah were straight, not warped and waved as I knew them, and stranger still, the step was gone. This gave me pause, but I forced myself on until I reached the actual wall of the cottage, and huddled against it. It felt clammy. I shivered in my lightweight clothing, hugging my arms about myself. The cold seeped up through the soles of my feet.

Someone was cooking. I lifted my head, sniffing, as the smell of meat drifted out from the cottage. I realised then that the window had no glass in it, just wooden shutters which fastened across what was otherwise an open square in the wall. And they weren't very well-made shutters, either. There were several gaps in them, and from the angle I was looking, I could see part of the ceiling inside the room.

It was not the ceiling I remembered. The

beams were exposed, thick and roughly cut, and I could see the dull gleam of a pottery jug, set snugly upon one of them. Carefully, inching my way, I raised myself until I could put my eye to one of the gaps. I don't know what I'd expected to see, but it wasn't this.

The white cat.

It was curled on the hearth before the fire, a classic cat pose. How had it got inside so fast? And how could it look so contented, when it had been the catalyst for something so catastrophic?

Footsteps. A man's arm appeared within my small sliver of vision. He placed a bowl of food beside the cat and it sat up, stretched, and began to eat with quick, delicate movements of teeth and tongue. The hand stroked the silky head with long fingers, and then withdrew.

Frustrated, I edged sideways to another gap in the shutters, and then another. My heart was no longer a steam train, it was an express, humming along the tracks. I found him. He had his back to me, but even so shock made my legs go wobbly. He was a big man, a very big man. The set of his shoulders under his blue shirt was broad and straight, although he stood slightly stooped at the moment—I realised he was too tall to stand up in that low room. He had dark hair, tied at his nape with a piece of ribbon. A ponytail.

Perhaps I made a noise, or perhaps he just sensed my presence, because quite suddenly he turned around.

I forgot the bitter cold. I forgot my terror and

confusion. I knew the man standing inside my cottage really was Devlin, the boatman.

Devlin was in my cottage. But this was no shadowy, insubstantial figure. This was no ghost. Devlin was a real flesh and blood man!

I could see the sheen on his skin and the dark shadow on his shaven jaw. I could see the hollows of his dark eyes and his wide, curving mouth. 'Dark of visage,' Howard had said in his book, and so he was. Dark and handsome.

I took a deep breath. If I didn't get a grip on myself, I was going to run screaming into the river. I took another deep breath, and opened my eyes.

Devlin had moved away, and I had to do another search of the cracks in the shutters to find him. He was stooping over a large box, or chest, which had been placed in the middle of the room. He was side on to me this time, and I took the opportunity of admiring his profile.

His clothing was strange—loose trousers of some thick, hard-wearing material, and a blue shirt. Both were unironed and well worn. He had boots on his feet and, as he knelt, I saw a hole in the sole of one of them that needed mending.

A gust of icy wind blasted around the corner, bringing with it rain and sleet, stinging my bare skin and making me shudder violently. This wasn't the sweet mellow autumn I had left behind; this was a bitter winter's night. I had slipped forward a couple of months and backwards God knows how many years!

Devlin was looking at the window again.

Perhaps he really did sense my presence beyond the shutters. He was staring straight at me and there was something so compelling and yet melancholy in his expression, I was drawn into it like a moth to a candle.

A hand gripped my nape in an excruciatingly painful hold. I gave a muffled shriek.

'Devlin!' a rough voice shouted. 'You've a spy 'ere, be God.'

Sounds from the cottage told me that the big man was moving towards the door. I struggled wildly, but whoever had me in his grip wasn't letting go, and I hung like a terrified kitten from the pinch of his thumb and fingers. He shook me slightly, as a warning, I suppose, not to try and escape.

I saw Devlin's boots in front of me. My eyes crept up, up, and then his face swooped down before mine. He'd bent over to peer at me. I saw the gleam of his dark eyes. His eyelashes flickered.

The man who had hold of me gave me another good shake, and finally let me go. I came down hard on my knees on the bricks and squealed with the pain of it. The two men spoke over the top of me.

'We can't 'ave spies, Devlin. She'll 'ave to go.'

'Go?' Devlin repeated in a voice like soft rain. 'Go where?'

'Into the river, maybe.'

But Devlin wasn't having that. He made a sound like a snort and reaching down, hauled me to my feet. His fingers were strong and warm ... and alive. He set me slightly behind him. 'This is no spy,' he said. 'I know her. She's Grandma Ducat's girl.'

'I s'pose she always comes callin' on you without her shift,' the voice retorted with sarcasm.

Trembling with shock and cold, I peeped out at the other man from under Devlin's massive forearm. I had half expected to see the brutal face of the convict who had called me Kate. But instead it was a man of medium size with stringy brown hair and a face full of teeth. He wore a soldier's uniform—I could see his buttons shining in the light from the door. He was watching me with narrowed eyes.

'You're the man, Devlin,' the soldier was saying grimly. 'It's your neck'll break if it goes wrong. I'll not stand up for you, you know that. I'll say I never met you, and they'll believe me above you.'

Devlin laughed a quiet laugh. 'I know it. Now, what have you to tell me? Me dinner's gone cold inside, or else the cat's got it.'

The two men moved together, heads close. The conversation was brief, but Devlin seemed pleased by it and nodded several times. The soldier turned to me again, and now his eyes feasted on my bare arms and legs.

'You're a mean bastard, Devlin,' he sneered, 'to let your woman go about like that. Buy her a shift!' And he slipped away into the freezing darkness and was gone.

This is madness, I thought, and then almost laughed aloud. It *was* madness. I had slid over the edge. They would find me when I didn't return to Melbourne, quite demented, seeing things, hearing things, gibbering to myself and a ghost called Devlin.

'You're not real, are you?' I asked his back with quiet desperation. I had passed beyond fear. I think I knew it was real, but I had to make some sort of token protest. I had to pretend disbelief. I felt I owed it to my own sanity. 'This is a hallucination, isn't it? I should have spoken to Bolten.'

He turned and looked down at me, his expression perplexed. He must have been a good two metres tall. And big with it. He blocked out the moon and the sky and everything else. He could pick me up with one hand and squeeze the life out of me, if he wanted to. But he didn't look as if he wanted to.

'Who's Bolten?' he asked me quietly.

'I ...' I waved my hand. 'It doesn't matter.'

'And who are you?' he added. 'I said you were Grandma Ducat's girl, but you're not. She's got more flesh on her than you,' and he smiled at some fleeting memory.

'Look,' I said, 'do we really have to go through this? I know you're not real.'

He frowned. 'You've a strange manner of speaking.'

So had he, only I wasn't so rude as to say so. He had a marked Irish lilt, but it had been tempered by his years in Van Diemen's Land into a crossbred accent I had never heard before, and which was probably long extinct.

'You're not real,' I said again, stubbornly.

'No?' He took a step towards me. I don't know what I expected him to do but it was only through sheer willpower that I stayed where I was. He reached out and touched my cheek, his fingers oddly gentle. I closed my eyes.

'You're cold,' he said, and there was nothing in his voice to tell me what he was thinking. 'Barnet was right, you need a shift, woman. Come inside and I'll find you one. Whatever possessed you to come out on such a night without your clothes? No, you can tell me inside.'

I opened my eyes. We looked at each other, there in the cold moonlight, and there was a sense of inevitability about the moment, and a sense of foreboding. And I wondered whether he felt it too.

Inside, the cottage seemed structurally the same. Here was the narrow passage running through to the back, the two front rooms leading off it. The back quarters were too dark to see. Devlin led me into the room I had been able to view through the gaps in the shutters. There was a fire crackling in the fireplace and with a great shudder I headed for it.

I heard the creak of the floor as Devlin moved about the room, but I huddled nearer to the fire trying to rub the life back into my arms and legs, and didn't turn. The floor was bare boards, and the rug in front of the hearth looked suspiciously like a piece of sacking. Suddenly something heavy and warm, a large coat, was placed about me. Automatically, I grasped at it, catching Devlin's hands in the process, where they rested lightly upon my shoulders.

'That'll warm you,' he said, and smiled down into my eyes.

I thought I might melt.

He moved away, over to a short, squat cupboard by the wall, and found a bowl among the clutter of eating utensils and brought it back to the table, rearranging things to make more room. I glanced nervously about me, taking note of the homemade table and benches; they had a rustic quality that had lately become so fashionable. Apart from the cupboard, the only other piece of furniture was a large trunk with its lid thrown back, which Devlin had been looking into when I peered at him through the shutters earlier.

I longed to go and poke and pry in it, but I knew that might be inadvisable on such short acquaintance.

Devlin had pulled out one of the benches and

nodded at the table. 'Come and eat,' he said. 'Then we can talk.'

I didn't know if I liked this 'we can talk' bit. What could I say to him? I'm from the future. Did you know that you'll disappear and never be seen again?

Holding the coat around me, I picked myself up and shuffled to the table. The bench was low and I landed on it with a bump. Devlin didn't say anything, just sat himself down beside me, but far enough away so that he could turn sideways and have a good look.

I wondered what he thought. I wasn't at my best, and unlike my public, he wouldn't be blinded with the notion that I was a 'star'. All he would see was a rather thin blonde with a pointed chin and brown Labrador eyes.

'Who are you?'

I glanced at him sideways. 'My name is Kate O'Hara,' I announced primly.

His eyes gleamed, but his mouth didn't smile. 'Ah,' he said. 'Well, Kate O'Hara, have you run off, is that it? Have you bolted from your master? Or is it your husband, then?'

I said nothing.

'Can you go back?' he asked, his voice dropping even lower. It raised the hairs on the back of my neck.

'I don't know,' I whispered, and that was true enough.

He nodded, pretending he understood. 'Eat up,' he said suddenly. He reached over and picked

122

up my bowl, and then ladled in something out of a crockery pot in the centre of the table, before replacing the bowl in front of me.

At least the mixture in the bowl *smelt* good, I thought, eyeing it suspiciously. But what was it? What did they eat in 1829? Was it 1829, the year of the fire? It looked like meat and a few vegetables, swimming in thin gravy. Carefully, I scooped some up on the wooden spoon Devlin had provided for me, and nibbled. Good! Not as much flavouring as I was used to, but well cooked and pleasant to the taste. Hot, too. The heat of it seeped through me, bringing a sting of colour to my cheeks. I took another nibble.

Devlin was watching me again. 'Kangaroo,' he offered. 'Better than your roast beef.'

I had tried kangaroo once or twice before in restaurants which specialised in Australian cuisine—a few slivers arranged on a white plate with one carrot and a couple of snow peas. It hadn't tasted like this. There was a lamp on the table, flickering and wavering and smoking slightly. This was the light I had seen through the shutters. Carefully, under cover of the table, I dug my nails into my knee until I drew blood. Nothing changed. Devlin kept eating steadily and the lamp kept smoking. Behind me, the fire burned warmly in the hearth—I could feel the lovely heat of it against my back—and outside the wind howled around the cottage and across the wild surface of the river. A curlew called, like a mourning lover. The sound made

Devlin lift his head and stare at the shuttered window.

His stillness affected my already heightened senses. 'What is it?' I asked nervously.

'The curlews. Someone or something's disturbing their nest. Could be a tiger, or a devil. Could be one of Cromarty's kangaroo dogs out for the night.'

'A tiger?' I yelped, and then realised he must be speaking of a Tasmanian Tiger, that dog-like creature with stripes, extinct in my time. And a Tasmanian Devil, a rather vicious little furry creature that could tear a man's hand off. Cromarty? Well, I had already met him.

'How far is the convict barracks from here?' I asked nonchalantly.

Devlin was ladling himself some more kangaroo stew. He had a loaf of flattish, coarse-looking bread beside him and, when he had finished ladling, he cut a slice like a doorstep and handed it to me.

'A mile through the bush, two by river,' he answered me. His eyes were dark and unreadable. 'Do you know someone there, Kate O'Hara?'

I knew Cromarty, and Major Dunwich, and one of the convicts, but I wasn't going to explain that to Devlin. I shook my head.

'You don't give much away, do you?' he half smiled. And then the curlew sounded again, and he turned back towards the window.

'Is it 1829?' I ventured.

'So they say.' He was indifferent.

'Has the fire happened yet?' I asked him, without meaning to, and then could have bitten my tongue.

He turned slowly and looked at me. 'Fire? What fire is that? There's been no fire that I know of.'

I didn't answer; I couldn't. I heard him sigh, and then he rose to his feet.

'I'll fetch you that shift, Kate O'Hara. You stay and finish your stew.'

Idiot! I told myself. You'd never make a spy, you'd blurt out the truth every time! But another part of my brain was thinking: I like the way he says my name. He speaks it the way it was meant to be spoken.

I watched him go out into the narrow passage. I could hear the creak of the floor and the rustle of clothing in the other room, as if he were rummaging through a chest or a drawer. My stomach felt pleasantly full, and I pushed aside my bowl and went over to the window, opening the shutters a fraction to look out.

There was the river, cold and grey with rain, and a glimpse of moonlight as the dark clouds fled across the sky. I closed the shutters with a shiver, and wandered across the little room towards the fireplace. I had to pass the trunk, and hesitated beside it. Giving in to the urge to pry, I peered in. It was full of Devlin's belongings—clothing, books with old-fashioned and unfamiliar titles. It was as if he were going on a holiday, and was busy packing the 1829 version of a suitcase.

I reached down and touched one of the books with my finger. The binding was stiff and worn, with cracks forming along the spine. There was a salty smell, as if the trunk had been to sea. Even more curious now, I crouched down and inspected the front of it. There were lots of bumps and scrapes, as if it had been heaved about in a ship's hold. Carefully, I eased the lid down, just enough to enable me to see the top of it. There was a name burned into the wood, so that the letters stood out.

It said, 'Thomas Devlin', and that was all.

Something moved to my left. The white cat sat on the far side of the hearth, watching me with its yellow eyes. I had forgotten all about it until now. But there it sat, as solid and real as ever. My fingers itched to reach out and touch it again, to see if what had happened before would happen again, but I was frightened. I froze, staring at it.

So ... what would happen if I did touch it? Would I be transported back to my own time, back to this exact same spot in the cottage? Or would I end up somewhere else, in some other time? I didn't want to know, not yet. I wanted to stay here.

Devlin's heavy footsteps came into the room. The cat stretched and approached him, winding itself about his boots. It peered between them at me with sly yellow eyes. He followed the direction of my gaze and I watched his mouth lift at the corners. 'I don't know where she came from, but she's mine now. When it suits her.'

He was carrying a bundle in the crook of one arm, and now held it out to me. I took it from him gingerly, keeping well away from the cat, and examined it. There was a brown dress, long-sleeved and long-skirted, very plain. The cloth felt thin with wear and washing. A long line of buttons fastened the back together, and the waist was so narrow I suspected it was meant to wear with some kind of corset. Fortunately, I was thin enough to do without.

As well as the dress, there was something like a long petticoat, which I assumed was the shift there had been so much fuss about, and some thick black woollen stockings—was this what a woman of fashion wore in 1829? Finally, there was a pair of brown shoes made of a type of leather I had never seen before.

'Kangaroo skin,' Devlin answered my puzzled look. 'You can put them on in the other room. I've lit the candle for you.'

Clutching the clothing and shoes to me, I went into the room opposite. It was my bedroom, or would be in the future. The bed was a box-like structure, with a chair by the window and a chest on the other side. Another of the sacking rugs kept my toes off the icy floor, but the shutters allowed gusts of bitter wind into the room. Hastily, without removing my shorts and T-shirt, I began to dress.

The shift and stockings I dealt with easily enough, but the dress was awkward. I pulled it down over my body and tugged the sleeves to my wrists. It fitted well, even with the layers underneath, but the buttons at the back were impossible to do up properly. I managed a few at the top and bottom, but those in the middle had to stay undone.

The cloth smelt faintly of musk. I wondered whose clothing it was. Devlin didn't strike me as the type to spend his private moments wandering about in women's clothing. Perhaps there was a Mrs Devlin somewhere, although according to Howard's book, Devlin lived alone, and so far Howard had done pretty well for himself in the historical accuracy department. In fact, I wished I had brought the book with me so that I could refer to it, a sort of how-to manual!

I picked up the shoes and slipped them on. They fitted—the kangaroo skin was soft and comfortable.

Back in the passage, I hesitated. I had a sudden urge to creep out through the door, out into the night. And then what? It was very dark out there, and very cold. Taking a deep breath, and cautiously negotiating my long skirts, I went back to Devlin.

He looked up at my entrance, his dark eyes sweeping over me in a manner that was certainly appreciative. I had had some looks in my time, some more sincere than others, but none had ever caused me quite the warm glow that Devlin's did. Just then, the curlew sounded again, even more plaintive than before.

'Cromarty's kangaroo dogs?' I whispered, my eyes still on his.

He smiled. 'This is a lonely place at night, Kate O'Hara. But I like to be alone. I've spent too much time with men whose company I didn't enjoy, and now I'm free I pick and choose my companions as carefully as a man eating a maggoty biscuit.'

'You were a convict,' I said, and then wondered if I should have.

But he didn't seem to mind. 'I was,' he replied. 'Fourteen years' transportation for an act of rebellion. I was lucky not to be hanged. The flame of injustice was burning in me in those days, but time has all but put it out. No-one in Van Diemen's Land cares about the injustice in Ireland, Kate. There's a fact for you.'

I wanted to touch his face, I wanted to kiss his mouth and make him forget. But I didn't move.

He put his hands to his eyes and rubbed them, as if he were too tired to think properly, and then gave me a hard look. I held my breath, waiting for him to demand my reasons for being here, to tell me it was time for me to go.

'Will you take my bed, Kate, or will you take the chair by the fire?'

Surprise and relief deflated me like a balloon. 'The chair,' I answered breathlessly. 'Thank you.'

He lifted his shoulders in a faint shrug, as if it were nothing. As if he allowed strange women to sleep in his home every night of the week. 'I'll say goodnight to you then.'

'Goodnight,' I whispered, but he had already gone, down the passage to the back of the cottage, into the darkness. There was the sound of another door opening and closing, and a burst of cold, damp air.

There's a door at the back, I told myself in amazement. That's where Devlin's ghost was going in the night, when he walked through the cottage. And that explained the bootprints that stopped at the back wall.

But it didn't explain much else.

9

'Devlin!'

The distant call woke me. I stretched, wriggling my toes in the warmth of the bed and snuggling down under the rough coverings. There was a male smell that was not unpleasant.

My eyes flew open. I was in Devlin's bed. I blinked, trying to clear my muddled thoughts. I didn't remember being transferred from the hard chair in front of the dying fire to the warmth of the bed, but obviously it had happened. I lifted the blankets and peered down at myself, and was relieved to find I still had the dress on, though minus the kangaroo skin shoes.

'Devlin!' The call came again, and this time I realised it was coming from the river's far shore. Carefully, I eased myself out of the bed, my feet flinching from the cold floorboards, and peered out of the shuttered window.

Someone had come into view. It was Devlin. He seemed even bigger than the previous night, if that was possible. I watched him stride down the bank towards the jetty where a boat was tied. He wore the same loose dark trousers, muddy boots and the thick coat I had slept in, only it was a jacket on him. There was a scarf around his throat in a loose knot, but his head was bare, his dark hair tied at his nape as before.

'I'll come over for you!' Devlin shouted, and his voice rang out across the water.

I searched about me for the shoes and finally found them in the chest in the corner. When I turned back to the window, I saw that Devlin was in the boat now. I watched him take up the oars, slip them into the rowlocks, and begin to row. Each stroke seemed to take him several metres, and the boat was soon in the middle of the river, and closing on his customer on the other side.

Something brushed against my skirts and the thick woollen stocking at my ankle. I looked down nervously, expecting to see a rat or a large spider, and froze. It was the cat, tail held aloft, making burbling noises in its throat as it butted me again in a timeless feline request for food.

Jerkily, I lifted my head and looked about. The window was still shuttered, and beyond the cottage Devlin was helping his customer into the boat. Nothing had changed; I hadn't jumped forward in time.

A weird combination of disappointment and relief gripped me, making me feel sick. I sat down abruptly on the chair by the window. It hadn't worked. Why? Had I been wrong, wasn't it the cat that had caused all this trouble in the first place? Was it something else? But although I racked my brains, there was nothing I could think of. It had been my touch on the cat that sent me spinning into Devlin's time. Why hadn't it done the same again?

'Perhaps I'm stranded here,' I whispered to myself.

The cat butted me again, reaching out one white paw to claw at my skirt.

'Watch it.' I looked down resentfully into the yellow eyes. I was tempted to kick it out of the way, but restrained myself. Who knew? Perhaps the cat could time travel at will. I'd better stay in its good books.

The sitting room smelled of smoke and last night's kangaroo stew. Devlin had set the fire again, and it was burning brightly. I was making a beeline for it, when the sound of voices interrupted me. I changed my mind and went to the door. Devlin had delivered his customer safely to this side of the river. I lurked in the passage and watched them through the open door.

'My thanks to you, Devlin!' the man said in a brisk voice. He was a short, portly gentleman, his large stomach stretching the fine silk of his blue and gold patterned waistcoat to its limits. He wore a dark coat, pinched in where his waist used to be, a dark neck scarf, and buff-coloured tight trousers over shining black boots. Beside Devlin, so huge and shaggy, he looked like a glossy little pony.

I had edged closer, so I could see better when he suddenly trotted towards the cottage. I thought he meant to come inside and quickly stepped back. The movement caught his eye and he stopped, mouth agape, staring at me.

'Well, who is this then?' he demanded in a meaningful sort of voice. 'Have you visitors, Devlin? Or is it that Ducat girl, eh? Is it you, Sally? Come out here, girl, and let me look at you.'

Devlin had reached the little man now, and stepped in front of him, trying to shield me from his view. 'She's shy, Mr Tuck.'

Mr Tuck! I thought with amazement. Was this short, fat man Howard Tuck?

Almost at once, I realised that it couldn't be. Howard had been a child in 1829. This must be his father, the fearless and respectable pioneer. I couldn't help a little smile.

'Shy?' Mr Tuck was ducking and diving, trying to see around Devlin. 'When has Sally ever been shy?' His florid face took on a sort of smirk, as if he should know. Not quite so respectable then, I amended. He had outmanoeuvred Devlin now, and was peering into the cottage. I knew he wouldn't be satisfied until he'd had a good look at me, so I took a deep breath and stepped outside. It was only then that I wondered what I must look like in the borrowed dress I'd slept in and my hair unbrushed. I watched his smirk turn to uncertainty.

'This isn't Sally!' he said crossly, turning to glare at Devlin as if it was his fault.

Perhaps, I thought, this is the time for a little respect and humility.

'My name is Kate O'Hara ... sir,' I said, and bobbed the curtsy I'd had to learn once for a play.

Mr Tuck straightened his waistcoat, pulling himself up to his full height. 'Kate, is it? I've not seen you about, Kate.'

'I've only lately arrived, sir,' I replied, eyes downcast modestly.

'Oh. Are you staying long?' Tuck seemed fascinated by me and moved closer. I felt his breath on my hair.

'I ... I don't know, sir. There is illness at home, you see,' and I made a little catch in my voice. I was really getting into this.

Tuck lifted a hand, as if to pat my shoulder, and then thought better of it. 'I'm sorry to hear of it, Kate. I'm very sorry to hear of it. Are you a relation of Mr Devlin here? I did not know he had any living in this colony.'

I flicked Devlin a look under my lashes.

'Kate is a cousin,' he said, and there was a glow in his dark eyes I couldn't read.

Mr Tuck had to be satisfied with that. He bade me good day, but turning to Devlin murmured, 'Peculiar accent, Devlin. Irish, is it? I can't say I've ever heard its like before.'

I didn't hear what Devlin replied. I went back inside the cottage and sank down in the chair by the fire, unsure my legs would hold me up any longer. The cat was curled on the hearth, eyes closed, smiling beneath its whiskers.

Again I resisted the temptation to kick it.

'Who are you?' Devlin was in the doorway, watching me, that gleam still in his eyes.

'I told you.' I met his gaze squarely. 'Kate O'Hara.'

'Then *what* are you, Kate O'Hara.'

'I'm an actress,' I confessed, and then wondered if I'd said the right thing. Until fairly recent times, actresses had been looked upon as the next rung up from prostitutes. How would Devlin take my admission?

He made a sound that could have been a laugh. 'And I should have guessed it!' he muttered. 'What are you doing in Leeward? There're no playhouses here. You'd do better to return to The Camp.'

I hesitated. 'I don't know what I'm doing here, Devlin. And I don't know whether I can go back.'

After a moment Devlin said softly, 'I'm not sure what to make of you, Kate O'Hara, but I find myself liking you anyway.'

I met his smiling eyes and thought: Yes, you're really something, Thomas Devlin. Sally

Ducat is a lucky girl to have you to cuddle up to at night.

Maybe he knew what I was thinking, because he laughed. It deepened the fine lines about his eyes and the deeper ones from his nose to his lips. As I watched him, the most wonderful feeling of contentment filled me. It was not like being with Ian, there was no contentment with Ian. Life had been like a ride on a ferris wheel, either up so high I felt I could grab the stars, or dropping so low I thought I would crash into the earth. Devlin was a different prospect, and I didn't want to let him go.

'Can I stay here a bit longer?' I asked diffidently, and held my breath on his answer.

It seemed a long time coming. 'I'd say yes to you, Kate O'Hara, but ... there's a thing I've set myself up to do, and who knows what will happen after.'

'What have you set yourself to do?' I asked him curiously.

But he wouldn't tell me and his face grew closed. 'Stay today and tonight,' he said quietly, instead. 'After that ... I can promise you nothing.'

There was finality in his voice, and now was not the time to argue with him.

The stew simmered quietly in the pot, and I lifted the lid and inspected it. Devlin was outside, busy rowing a couple of soldiers across the river. Their horses swam beside the boat, floundering and snorting in the cold water. But the soldiers did not want their uniforms wet, and I could not blame them.

They climbed out of the boat onto the wooden jetty, and Devlin walked with them along the riverbank, where they remounted and vanished into the bush. There seemed to be a track there, formed through constant use.

How much longer to go until the night of the fire? I asked myself. How many days or weeks until Devlin disappears from the history books as if he had never been?

The cat was sitting on one of the chairs, watching me calmly. I stared back at it, wondering how it would be if I were to return to my time now. And never see Devlin again and never know what had happened to him.

The feeling of loss was so intense I folded my arms across my stomach, as if to keep in the pain. I couldn't leave, whatever the consequences. I didn't want to.

There was the beginning of a thumping ache behind my eyes, reminding me I had left my medication behind. I contemplated with a hollow feeling how long it would take for the headache to become excruciating.

It didn't take long.

By the time the stew was ready, I had reached that stage where the light jabbed like needles into my eyes. I tried to lift my head and felt pain strike at my skull, dull blows, never ending. Like a coiled monster beginning to wake, the headache gathered strength. It knew, somehow, it knew I had no defences.

'What is it, Kate?' Devlin was there, and I hadn't even heard him come in.

'Headache,' I whispered. Even uttering that one word hurt.

I felt him move closer, and then his hand brushed my forehead. His fingers stroked, finding the pulse. He stood behind my chair, and I felt his hands rest a moment on my crown.

'When I was taken by the soldiers, they knocked me down with a rifle butt to my head,' he said softly. 'I used to have pains in it so bad, Kate O'Hara, I wished I could die. Are yours like that then?'

I nodded once, and felt the jar of it all the way to my toes.

'Danny had the touch. He could take the pain away with his hands. Will you let me do what he did? Will I smooth away the pain?'

I stirred uneasily. What did they use to cure illness in these days? Leeches and opium? And then the volume knob in my head turned up a notch and I gave up fighting. 'Yes,' I gasped and closed my eyes.

His fingers began to touch, gently, so light it was hardly massage, more a caressing of my skull. He found the place, above my ear, where I had cut my head on the car door during the accident. The raised scar was still there, hidden by my hair.

'You've been hurt.' Devlin's soft voice enfolded me, like the warmth from the fire. 'Sit still here, sit still now, and I'll take away the hurt, sweet Kate.'

Sweet Kate. The warmth grew inside me, spreading out to encompass every cell, every pore. I began to lose the ability to think. To keep myself lucid, I grasped at something he had said.

'Danny? Who is Danny?'

His fingers kept moving; I felt like purring. I really didn't care whether he answered me or not.

'Danny was my friend. We grew up together, and we dreamed of freedom. Danny's grandfather was a "white boy" and his father took part in the great Rebellion of 1798, and was hanged for it. Danny's uncle was one of Emmet's men in 1803, one of the United Irishmen who tried to march on Dublin Castle, and failed. We had the same thoughts and the same dreams. We'd lead the charge. It was Danny heard of the plan to take Dublin Castle, and do what Emmet failed in. But it got no further than talk, and talk was enough to arrest us. Danny had a book he always carried. He had written things in it—I know he meant none of it, but the saying was enough. It was full of the stuff he'd heard all his life, the sort of rough justice his grandfather had held with. We were sent to the gaol. I was sick from the blow to my head, and the pains started. Without Danny, I would have taken my own life, just to stop them. I wanted to die, but Danny kept me alive. "We'll stand together," he said. "We'll stand together, Thomas! If we're together, no evil can befall us!" And I believed him. We sailed together to Van Diemen's Land, and we survived it. It began to seem as if, as long as we were together, we'd be safe. I was his talisman, and he was mine. But when we reached Hobart Town, Danny was assigned to a master in Jericho, and I was sent to one in New Norfolk.'

He paused, as though the memories were here in the room with us. Through my haze of pain I imagined the two young men, friends from boyhood, arrested and thrown into prison then transported across the world to Tasmania. How they must have suffered! But that friendship had become their strength, their bond ... How traumatic must separation have been?

'I managed well enough,' Devlin said at last. 'I can hold my anger inside me, if I have to. But Danny was not good at that. His temper was always the master of him, so quick it was away before he could fasten it down. He was into trouble time and time again. In six years I had my ticket-of-leave, and was working for myself part of the time. I was a waterman at The Camp, carrying passengers from the ships to the shore, and then I signed on to the whale boats for a season, down in the icy southern seas. But there wasn't a day when I didn't think of Danny, and how he was faring. When I reached Hobart Town again, I tried to find him.'

'And did you?' I whispered, or was I only thinking it?

His fingers smoothed the hair back from my brow, stroking soft, now hard, as if drawing the stubborn pain away. My body was liquid, without substance.

'I found him,' he said. 'He was in the Campbell Street Gaol again, sent back there by his master for insolence, and it was not the first time. It seemed as if he was back every couple of months for one thing or another. He spent some time on the wharves, in the iron gang there, and was taken up again for fighting. I saw him in the gaol, waiting for his trial, and though he was bruised and hardened, there was still the Danny I knew in his eyes.

'I was away again after that, sailing a cutter out of Half Moon Bay. There was a storm blew up which nearly drowned me, but this isn't the time to tell of that. When I came back to Hobart Town, Danny was gone. They'd sent him into Macquarie Harbour this time. Hell's Gates. I've heard men talk about that place—working in water up to their waists, felling trees and hauling logs and the rain never stopping, never—I didn't think I'd ever see him again. I met a girl in Hobart Town, and it was she who brought me to Leeward. I took up the job here of boatman, and it was like coming home. The girl, she took up with a sheep farmer and went to live with him. That's her shift you're wearing, sweet Kate. She said she didn't want her old clothes—he was rich enough to buy her everything new.'

I could barely keep my eyes open, but I didn't

want to sleep. I wanted to listen to Devlin.

'I stayed here, I was happy here in a way I hadn't been for a long time. One day, I was out on the river, out near the convict barracks. There were a couple of men from the iron gang, chopping wood and putting it into those carts they pull. I wasn't looking at them. I never look those men in the eyes, because I know ... I know. And then someone said my name, soft and slow, as if it was a word they'd almost forgotten. And it was Danny.'

His voice stopped. I felt my thoughts drifting, like the river, twirling and swirling in little eddies. I don't think I slept, but neither was I awake. It was something between the two. I saw Ian, sitting in the corner. He was drinking whisky from a glass, and he raised it to me in a toast. He was smiling. He said, *Forgive me, Kate?* I felt myself smiling back. It was as if we were saying goodbye.

Devlin moved to place another log on the fire and his foot brushed my skirts. Devlin, I thought, Devlin, and his name was a chant which brought me up from wherever I had been. I opened my eyes and found him watching me.

'How is it now?'

I smiled up at him. 'Wonderful,' I whispered, and stretched. My body was like flotsam, floating in a calm ocean. Whatever was in Devlin's fingers should be patented and sold as a miracle cure. My headache was completely gone.

I stood up, and swayed. He caught me, and as if we couldn't help it, we strained against each other. My breath stopped. I was melting and Devlin was the fire. I put my hand up to his face and he turned his mouth into my palm.

'Kate,' he murmured. His fingers lifted to encircle my throat and his big, blunt thumb stroked my pulse, backwards and forwards. I rubbed my cheek against his hand.

He lifted me up. The shutters in the bedroom were wide open to the chill air, but he left them open as if he didn't give a damn what anyone thought. I liked the way he left them open. He placed me gently on the bed, and then his hands were on my body. He slid them under my skirts and found the tops of my woollen stockings. There was something incredibly sexy about the way he drew them down over my thighs. I pulled him down on top of me, and felt the rough cloth of his trousers against my bare legs. His mouth was on mine, and I wrapped my legs around his hips, feeling the hard length of him against my own flesh.

'I want to love you, Kate O'Hara,' he said.

Outside, a voice on the opposite bank called for Devlin to come over, but he ignored it.

'I took advantage of you,' he said softly, stroking my hair.

I turned to look at him in amazement. My head was resting against his shoulder, his arm cuddling me close. My voice was dry. 'I'd say it was the other way around.'

'Would you say that?' he mocked.

I rolled over and lay on top of him. I gazed down into his face, touching it, searching it with eyes and lips and fingers, loving it ... and knowing I would never be able to get enough of him. 'Devlin,' I whispered, 'it was something that would have happened between us anyway.'

He tasted my lips in a long kiss.

The voice had stopped calling. A customer lost, I thought wryly. I was bad for business. 'How did you become a ... a boatman?' I asked him, propping myself up on my elbows, the better to gaze down into his wonderful face. His eyes were far away.

'I know the water,' he told me softly, at last. 'I know the ways of it. My father was a waterman, and his father before him. It's in my blood. Sometimes, I stand and look at the river, and I feel as if I am a part of it and it is a part of me.'

I had felt that too. The river bound us in different ways and yet in similar ways. 'Will you always stay here?' I asked him. 'With the river?'

He touched my cheek, his fingers like magic. 'If I had a choice, I would stay, but there's something I must do, and the doing of it might cost me my freedom again.'

His words made me shiver. 'What must you do? What do you mean?'

He hesitated, and then drew me down beside him, holding me so that I couldn't look into his face. His voice was a warm whisper in my ear.

"I wanted to weep when I saw Danny in the iron gang at the barracks here—or what used to be him. He'll be a dead man if I don't free him from that place. Do you understand me now? Do you see why you can't stay here with me?'

His words spiralled in my mind, cutting through the clouds of euphoria. My breath was ragged, as ragged as his against my ear. I shivered, and his arms tightened about me.

I turned and kissed him. He nuzzled my neck with his rough chin and warm lips. 'There's nothing for me at home,' I told him, and my voice was trembling.

'Why is it you've come now?' he asked, and he sounded angry and sad and bitter, all at once.

'Perhaps I've come to help you free Danny,' I whispered.

10

Devlin and I were eating our evening meal when Barnet turned up to see Devlin. He stood against the cold evening light, eyeing me from the doorway with a dangerous look.

'You still here?' he asked, a nasty sneer in his voice. 'Looks like you've found another stray she-cat, eh Devlin?'

Devlin didn't seem particularly amused, although he answered calmly enough. 'What have you to tell me, Barnet?'

Barnet smiled at him, evidently reading

something in his face that I couldn't. 'I'll be on guard duty tomorrow night, that's what I've come to tell you, Devlin. And after that, I'm off to Hobart Town for a stint there. So it's tomorrow night, or it's not at all.'

There was a silence, and I watched Devlin's face, blank and still, while beneath it his thoughts must be seething. 'Then it surely is tomorrow night,' he murmured at last.

'I'll need some coin for the drink,' Barnet said. 'It don't need to be anythin' fancy. The boys'll drink anything, long as it does the job.'

Devlin nodded as if he hadn't heard.

Barnet jerked his head in my direction. 'What about her? Is she goin' to come and play games with Cromarty, to take his mind off what's happenin' in the cells?'

Devlin looked down at him, and something in that look made Barnet back up a couple of steps. 'The prisoner knows what's to happen?' he asked evenly. 'You've spoken with him?'

Barnet nodded sulkily. 'He knows. If the drink does the trick, I'll 'ave him out by ten and you'll be waitin' on the river. No-one'll even know he's gone until mornin', and by then I'll be as drunk as the rest. Speakin' of which ...' He held out his hand.

Devlin took a leather drawstring purse from his pocket and opened it. He shook out some coins, as strange a collection as I'd ever seen, one with a hole punched in the middle and the rest all different shapes and sizes. He held them towards the other man, who snatched them and swiftly pocketed them.

'The rest you'll get when it's over,' he said.

But Barnet shook his head. 'Bring it with you,' he replied, and there was a sharpness in his eyes. 'If you're caught, I'll get nothin'. I want me money on the night, or I'll yell me head off.'

Devlin nodded slowly, as if he agreed with the sentiment. 'On the night then. When you deliver Danny to the boat, I'll hand you the money.'

Barnet turned to go, and we followed him outside. He hesitated. 'There's somethin' else. Major Dunwich is makin' one of his inspections of the bloody roads. He's due at the barracks in the next day or two, but no-one knows when. If he comes tomorrow … will I still go on with it? It'll be more dangerous.'

I felt my stomach dropping away towards my feet. Dunwich was coming. Dunwich had been there the night of the fire. This was beginning to feel very ominous.

'Yes,' Devlin was saying, 'we still go on with it.'

Barnet smirked and strode off along the rough path through the bush. Somewhere I could hear an axe ringing in the forest. Across the river, where in my time the land had been cleared and farmed, was more forest. I had an inkling of how the first white pioneers must have felt, all alone in this wilderness. And how Devlin must have felt, forcibly brought from his home in Ireland and transplanted in a foreign land.

So many of the convicts, like Danny, had been destroyed by their experiences, but not Devlin. Was the explanation for that in a man's basic personality … the type of man he had been born? Danny, with his fiery temper and dreams of freedom, and Devlin, big and calm and patient, who could sway with the wind and not rail against it.

'Do you really trust that man?' I asked Devlin, as Barnet's footsteps faded into the bush towards the convict barracks.

He smiled. 'I trust his greed.'

'What is this plan of yours?' He hadn't told me yet, but now I needed to know.

'Barnet is going to get the soldiers drunk, and pretend he's drunk himself. He'll be on guard duty tomorrow night, so it's his job to check on the prisoners, all locked up tight in their cells. He'll let Danny out, when it's safe, and take him down to the river where I'll be waiting with the boat. Then I'll bring him back here, fit him up into some new clothes, and take him south by river to Hobart Town. They won't expect that, they'll be thinking he'll go north to the wild country, to hide. And while they're searching north we'll find a ship to take us away.'

I didn't like the 'away' bit, but I put that aside. The plan itself sounded simple enough, apart from a few considerations. 'What about the overseer, Cromarty?' I ventured.

'Cromarty has separate quarters, and he drinks. He won't hear a thing.'

'And Major Dunwich?'

'I don't know Major Dunwich, but he's a friend of Governor Arthur, and that's enough for me. He'll do his duty, and then pen half-a-dozen reports to prove it. We'll just have to hope that Dunwich doesn't turn up until it's all over.'

'Devlin ...' But I didn't know what to say. How could I explain to him that I knew what was going to happen? There would be a fire, and the convicts would be captured again, and Devlin would disappear completely and forever. How did one tell a man in 1829 what we knew of his time from so far in the future?

I was a coward, and I couldn't do it.

The darkness was creeping across the river, the water still and smooth as a silver sheet, with only the faintest ripple. 'I want to come and get Danny with you,' I said.

He smiled and shook his head, but I caught his hand and held it tight, gazing into his face. 'You must let me come. If you take Danny away, I won't see you again for ... I won't see you again.'

What would happen to me once Devlin had gone? I hadn't thought of it before. I would be abandoned here, in a time I didn't know and probably wouldn't survive in. Would the cat take me back to my own time? Would I ever get back?

He put his hand to my neck and encircled it, caressing the pulse as he had done before. I could see he knew he should refuse me, make me stay and wait in the cottage like a good little woman.

But he *wanted* me beside him. The wanting part won.

I woke in the darkness, and listened to the wind in the trees beyond the river, and the curlew's mournful cry. Devlin lay sleeping beside me. The white blur of the cat caught my eye as it strolled past the room.

I hadn't seen much of it and understandably had avoided it. Devlin fed it and dealt with it; he seemed to love it. I wondered what would happen to it when he was gone.

There was a sound outside, a scraping sound that made me think of the bow of the boat on the riverbank. I sat up in the darkness, blinking, my breath a white mist from the cold. Slowly, shrinking from the chill, I edged out of the warm bed and went to peer through the shutters.

There was a figure in the darkness, stooped over the boat. Suddenly Devlin's big warm body was behind me, his arm slipping crosswise over my shoulder and about my waist. 'What is it?' he murmured.

'There's someone there.'

He looked past me, and then moved back to fetch his trousers and pull them on. He went out into the passage and I heard the faint click of the door opening. The figure at the boat must have heard, too, because his head came up, and he made as if to run. But Devlin was too fast for him, and in a very few strides was close enough to reach out and grasp an arm.

'No, no, let me go!' a voice cried. My breath went out in a sigh of relief. It was a boy, and a young boy by the sound of it. Devlin was dragging his unwilling captive towards the cottage. I found the candle and, with difficulty and little expertise, lit it from the coals of the fire in the other room.

Devlin slammed the door open and, holding fast to the wriggling boy, sat down on the bench by the table. 'Bring the light closer!' he shouted above the yells and complaints, and I came forward while Devlin grabbed a handful of the boy's hair and tilted his face to the light. He *was* young —about eight—with hair the colour of mud and eyes to match, bright now with tears of anger and fright.

Devlin laughed. 'It's Tuck's youngest!' And he gave him a shake and let him go. 'What are you doing here, boy? You're no sailor.'

My hand trembled, and the candle went out. Devlin swore softly, and the boy made a dart for the door and instead cannoned into me. I wrapped my arms about him, more from reflex than any wish to keep him. 'Howard?' I gasped. 'Howard Tuck?'

He went still. I felt him breathing quickly, like a trapped animal. And then his voice, high and tremulous, 'How do you know my name?'

My nerves had steadied. I let him go, but this time he didn't try to get away. Devlin was lighting the oil lamp on the table, the glow of it slanting across his naked back and shoulders. He turned slightly, and I saw the shine of his dark eyes on me.

'I read it somewhere,' I said lamely.

Howard peered at me suspiciously. 'Not from me Ma? You didn't hear it from her, did you? It's not true what she says. I'm not bad.'

He was standing straight, gazing up at me, his head thrown back, his pose all bravado. But his eyes were full of worried vulnerability. Suddenly, to my astonishment, I realised I liked Howard Tuck very much.

'No, it wasn't your Ma,' I assured him softly. 'And I don't think you're bad either, although,' I heard Devlin clear his throat, 'it isn't right to take things that don't belong to you. Mr Devlin needs his boat to bring people across the river. Why, he brought your father only the other day.'

Howard's look darkened. 'Pa's gone off to The Camp,' he announced, 'to be with one of his fancy ladies. That's what Ma says. We don't care if he never comes back.' He paused, and I saw the beginning of a thought shine in his eyes. 'Are you a fancy lady, ma'am?'

Devlin reached out then, and put his arm about me. 'She's as fancy as they come, Howard.'

Howard looked pleased by that.

'If you promise not to come out here at night again, I'll take you for a row one day,' Devlin went on thoughtfully, 'but I don't know if you have the strength of character to promise such a thing.'

Howard puffed himself up. 'That's an easy promise!'

'Well, then it's a deal between us.' Devlin held out his hand and after only a brief hesitation, Howard put his small one into it. They shook.

'You'd better go home now,' I said gently. 'Your Ma might be worrying. With your Pa gone she probably needs you more than ever.'

He nodded as if this were an undisputed fact, and turned to go. One more glance from the doorway, and then I heard him running along the riverbank and into the silence. 'I think we know now what's been disturbing the curlews,' Devlin announced. 'Young Howard has a name for wildness, but he's not so bad as his Ma says. The older brothers bully him, and his father's never there. Mrs Tuck just about runs the farm alone.'

I felt sad, hearing this. All that I had read about Howard's family was a lie, a lie which Howard had fabricated. He had turned his unhappy childhood into a happy one. The sadness turned to admiration. Well, I thought, good for him! I wished I was able to tell him his book was now a bestseller in Leeward.

'How *did* you know the boy's name, Kate?' Devlin was watching me, his eyes narrowed with curiosity.

But I was ready for him now. 'I heard it as I was passing through Leeward,' I said airily, and bent to rub my cold hands before the fading fire.

He said nothing, and I pretended that nothing more need be said. And then his arms closed about me and he pulled me back against his body. 'You're lying, Kate,' he said, cupping my breasts.

'No,' I gasped and lifted my face for his kiss.

His mouth hovered, teasing. 'You're lying,' he whispered, 'but I don't care. I know you as I know myself, and I'd trust you with my life.'

I touched his cheek. 'I love you, Devlin,' I told him with a sort of wonder.

'I know,' he said.

Just as dawn was breaking, I rose from the bed to fetch myself some water. There was a film of frost on the shutters and my breath was as cloudy as Dixie's cigarette smoke. Out on the river, the mist hung over the water, as though it were steaming hot instead of icy cold. The sky was soft steel with pink at the edges.

I drank the water, watching the sun rising. I realised, with a contradictory sense of great sadness, that I had never been so happy. I had found a place I loved and a man with whom to spend my life. And tonight I was going to lose him forever, and I didn't know how or why, and I didn't know whether I could stop it and change history, but I meant to try.

Would it help to tell Devlin about the fire? Or would it make things worse? It certainly wouldn't stop him from going to get Danny, I knew that. If I did tell him, who could say whether or not he would believe me? If the roles were reversed, I knew I'd have a bit of difficulty believing me, and I had all the advances of the twentieth century behind me. He was barely into the nineteenth. He might well listen, decide I was stark staring mad, and leave me behind.

I pressed my fingers to my eyes, wishing I could do something. Why was I here, if not to do something? I sighed. At least by sticking close to Devlin, I was in a position to help him if anything did go wrong—I had to comfort myself with that.

The cat was waiting for me in the passage and I glanced at it nervously over my shoulder. It followed me back into the bedroom, and jumped up onto the covers, kneading itself a comfortable spot on Devlin's feet. He half woke, flinging out an arm to draw me in. I snuggled up, warming myself, and watched the white cat, disgruntled by the movement, twitch its tail.

The yellow eyes had an almost malicious cast to them. It picked its way across the bedclothes towards me. My hand lay outside the covers, and the cat watched it expectantly. Almost against my will, and certainly against my better judgment, I reached out and touched the silky coat.

There was a buzzing in my head.

I was lying in my bed, alone, and the cottage was as quiet as the grave. My clock ticked on the dressing table, and far away an aeroplane was circling in the clear, blue autumn sky.

'Oh God, no!' I burst out, and sat up, shaking. I was wearing the shift Devlin had given me, but nothing else. Devlin's big, warm body was gone, left behind, long dead and turned to dust. The realisation was like someone tearing me in two.

I caught sight of the cat by the door, watching me. With a wordless cry, I lunged at it … and missed. It fled, out into the passage. 'Come back!' I screamed at it, but that only made things worse. It was in the sitting room now, on the hearth, the place where it spent so many of its hours in Devlin's time.

Above the mantelpiece, the painting caught the light from the window, making it seem as if it had a life of its own. Spellbound, I couldn't help but gaze up at it. Devlin, his head bent, pulling on the oars, and the woman with her hand trailing in the water. The scene was idyllic … Would I ever see him again, apart from in a painting?

Tears stung my eyes.

The cat was viewing me uncertainly, wondering if I was going to start yelling again. Slowly I inched forward towards it. Outside, the river slapped the bank, as empty as the cottage. *Devlin, oh Devlin.* The cat began to wash itself, nervous little licks. 'Please,' I whispered, and held out my hand. There were tears on my cheeks, I felt their warm saltiness. 'Please …' My fingers stretched out, trembling uncontrollably, and touched the animal's shoulder. I closed my eyes.

When I opened them again, I was standing before Devlin's dying fire, alone. Behind me, the winter light poked chilly fingers through the gaps in the shutters. More tears trickled down my cheeks. Now I wept for what might have happened and what might still happen—the unknown future.

After a time, I wiped my face. Why had this occurred now, when before the cat brushed my skirts and nothing happened? Had I been right when I thought the cat might control the time travelling? Or was there something more, something I hadn't remembered? I took myself back over the events of the past days ... and I realised what I should have known before. I was only able to travel through time when the cat touched my bare skin. When it brushed against my stockings or skirt, nothing happened.

I went back to bed, although it was really time to get up. But I wanted to lie beside Devlin, I needed to be held by him. I needed him very badly.

11

The steely dawn had given way to a cold, grey day. Devlin had heated water in various pots, a flotilla on the grid over the flames, enough for me to wash in. I had soaped myself all over with the coarse ball of soap he had proudly produced.

Devlin didn't believe in hot water. 'I bathe in the river,' he'd informed me, and then laughed at my look of horror. 'It's not cold, if you're quick.'

'I don't believe you,' I retorted. 'No-one could swim in there this time of year and live to tell about it.'

His smile grew. 'Could they not?' From the window, I watched him stroll barefoot down the riverbank, stripping off his shirt and tossing it aside, and then his trousers. He wore nothing underneath. He stood a moment, long enough to give me a good look at a body that I had to admit was truly magnificent, and then dived neatly into the river.

I caught my breath in sympathy. His dark head surfaced, and he shook the water from his hair. I saw his smile as he looked back to the cottage, and me at the window. 'Come in, Kate!' he shouted.

'No!' I shouted back, and then shook my head vigorously in case he couldn't hear me. Shivering from the chilly breeze which was coming in the window, I pulled my shift over my head, and gave my wet hair a good rub with the cloth I was using as a towel.

'Oh for electricity,' I murmured. 'Oh for gas! Hot water, straight from the tap, and central heating at the touch of a button, a washing machine, and an oven with—'

'Do you mean to catch your death there, ma'am?' The voice shocked me. I turned, slowly, and found my face centimetres from Duncan Cromarty's. He was standing at the window looking in, his little eyes all over me. Instinctively I snatched up my dress and held it against me.

Cromarty laughed soundlessly. 'Don't cover up on my account,' he said softly, with a look of complete disinterest.

It was the face I remembered from the night of the fire. The bloated features, the piggy eyes. He wore a plain brown waistcoat and a brown jacket over it, and both had a lot to cover. Cromarty was a tall man, and to look so fat he must have been terribly overweight. Some fat men are jolly. There was nothing jolly about Cromarty. I had an overwhelming sense of how evil he was. The smell of it hung about him, sour, contaminating.

For a moment I wondered why he didn't recognise me, and then I remembered that of course the night of the fire hadn't happened yet, although I very much feared it was about to. I tried to smile, tucking my damp hair back behind my ears.

'Oh, you startled me!' I said, in my best 'breathless maiden' voice.

Beyond Cromarty, Devlin had climbed from the river and gave himself another shake, like a very big dog. As I watched, he began to pull on his trousers. His skin was wet and tinged blue from the cold. Cromarty had seen the direction of my gaze and turned to see what I was looking at.

He froze.

I heard his breath wheeze between his lips, and glanced at him uneasily. He had turned an unpleasant mottled red, and now he muttered something under his breath I did not properly catch.

'What was that, Mr Cromarty?'

The piggy eyes swung around. 'How do you know me name?'

Startled by his sharp tone as much as his odd behaviour, I stood with my mouth ajar. He leaned closer. My skin crawled. 'Do you please your man, whore? I've sometimes wondered if the boatman was the sort o' man to take a woman or a man—seems he's the former. Meself, I see no use for your kind.' His gaze slid over me scornfully, and I knew he meant what he said. Cromarty was not interested in *my* body, he was interested in Devlin's.

Devlin, dressed now, ambled up to Cromarty, his expression pleasantly inquiring. 'You're wanting to go over the river then, Mr Cromarty?'

Cromarty leaned back on the window sill, effectively cutting me out of the conversation. 'Aye, I am, Devlin. One of the sheep farmers o'er there is to meet me. He wants some felons to clear his land.' Cromarty winked. 'I told him it's not somethin' Governor Arthur looks kindly on, but me ... I'm a different matter!'

Angrily, I pulled on my gown. I heard Devlin telling the overseer he had only to put on his boots, and Cromarty making some rejoinder. The greasy voice I had remembered from the fire was gone. Cromarty was much more certain of himself today, or else he did not feel he had to grovel to such as Devlin and me. The real Cromarty was staring out of those little eyes, and every instinct was telling me to beware.

Devlin came into the cottage and cocked an

eyebrow at my flushed and furious face. He grasped my shoulders, spun me around, and began to do up my buttons. 'He's a pig of a man,' he said softly into my hair. 'Did he insult you, sweet Kate?'

'Not me, not really. He insulted you.'

I heard him laugh, a little warm breath of sound on my nape, and then he had finished the buttons. 'I'll take you across now, sir!' he shouted, so that Cromarty could hear from outside. 'And maybe I'll drown you in the process,' he added in an undervoice, giving my ribs a squeeze. His hair, still wet, brushed my cheek.

'I wish you would,' I murmured grimly, and shivered.

I watched from the window. Cromarty climbed into the boat and Devlin pushed it out, scrambling in at the last moment. Cromarty leaned back, arms folded on his paunch, as if this were the Thames and he was Henry the Eighth. Devlin rowed, the muscles in his arms straining with each pull of the oars. God, but he was beautiful, and I couldn't blame others for thinking so, too. But the thought of Cromarty ...

Other thoughts followed. Did Cromarty abuse his position as overseer of the convict barracks? Of course he did. The dark tales of the convict chain gangs were full of hints of sodomy and homosexual rape. It was a predominantly male existence in the penal colonies. Lots of men with few women to soften their lives. But Cromarty ... it didn't matter about his sexual preferences, the man himself was evil. I didn't want to think about what may have happened to Danny.

Devlin reached the opposite shore, and Cromarty climbed out. He bent down then, to speak to him, and Devlin listened, staring out across the river, his wet hair falling loose about his shoulders. And then he made some reply, and began to row back. Cromarty stood on the other side, watching him with a rigid intensity that bespoke anger, before he walked away.

'Perhaps he'll die in the fire,' I told myself hopefully. But I already knew that Cromarty would survive.

'What did he say?' I asked Devlin when he had moored the boat and strode up to the cottage.

He gave me a look. 'Nothing I've not heard before, Kate darlin'.' But there was something in his face and his voice that caught in my chest.

'Come here,' I said softly, 'and I'll comb your hair for you.'

When he was seated, I drew the wide-toothed comb gently through the thick, dark strands. He sighed, and closed his eyes. 'Danny was an angel,' he murmured. 'He didn't deserve to be put in the power of a man like Cromarty.'

'A lot of people suffer cruelty and don't deserve it.'

He sighed again, silent while I combed.

'Are you thinking of tonight?' I asked him.

'I am.'

'Are you afraid?'

165

He made a little movement of his mouth. 'Not for myself, no. But for Danny, and for you.'

'I'm coming with you.'

He tried to turn and look at me, but I held his head and wouldn't let him. 'To get Danny?' he asked, puzzled. 'I know that. I said you could.'

'I'm coming with you afterwards.'

'No.'

I placed my palms against his temples, sliding them down over the strong planes of his face. I pressed my lips to the crown of his head. 'I must go,' I said, and my voice grated with need and longing. 'I can't live without you, Devlin. I'd rather die with you, than live safe here. God help me, I'd rather you killed me now. Drown me in the river! But don't leave me alone without you ...'

He turned and caught me in his arms, lifting me onto his lap and cradling me there. 'Kate,' he breathed. 'Men and women don't die of being alone. I know this, I *know* it.'

And he would, too. He knew it, just as I did.

'I'll follow you,' I told him, trying not to cry. 'I was the best Brownie they ever had! I can track you from here to the sea, if need be. And I will.'

He rocked me gently, bending to kiss my mouth, his hair swinging forward to curtain our faces. 'Darlin', darlin' Kate, I might die on the river, if I don't die beforehand. And it would hurt me more than dyin', if I thought I'd taken you into danger, and then left you to face it alone. I can't do that, do you see? I can't. I want you to be safe. As long as you live, then I live, too.'

'Why didn't we meet long ago?' I cried.

'I'll come back for you,' he whispered. 'You must wait for me here, Kate, so that I can find you. When I have a place for Danny and myself, I'll come for you and bring you to us.'

How? my mind screamed. How will you find me, when I don't know myself which century I will be in? But I said, 'Yes,' in a little, miserable voice.

He began to kiss me, small comforting kisses, and between each one he said, 'I'll come for you,' until the kisses grew longer and deeper and more passionate, and I no longer heard the words.

It was so dark, I could hardly see my hand in front of my face. We had gone to bed, not to sleep, but to lie in each others arms. Now it was late, and every second that passed drew me closer to all I feared. I had found the love of my life in circumstances so incredible, I still hardly believed them. A man I felt I knew as well as myself, a man as different from Ian as he could possibly be. And I was going to lose him.

Devlin leaned over me, and I felt his breath tickle my ear. I thought my heart would burst.

'We have to go now, Kate.'

I shivered and nodded my head.

'Do you still want to come?'

'Yes,' I said, and closed my mouth hard in case my teeth started to chatter.

'Good,' he murmured, and held me tight against him. 'I need you, sweet Kate. Put your clothes on, and the cloak. Do that now, darlin',' while I get the boat ready.'

I dressed and pulled the cloak around my shoulders, feeling its warm weight enclose me. Devlin had gone to Leeward in the afternoon and returned with it under his arm, a great billowing garment of woollen cloth lined with possum fur. When he gave it to me, I was more touched than I had ever been when Ian gave me expensive gifts.

Devlin was outside at the boat, and I went to join him. There was a gleaming thumbnail of a moon, peeping over the clouds. The mist on the river lay thick and still, only the gentle wash along the shore to show it was moving at all. It crept like awkward fingers around us, every movement sending it scuttling back from our feet and the hem of my cloak.

Steam drifted from Devlin's mouth whenever he breathed. He smiled and held out his hand to me. His fingers were warm and alive, and I knew I would never forget the feel of them.

The boat rocked as I settled myself in the stern, and then Devlin gave it a shove, out into the river, hauling himself in as it went. It rocked more from his movements than it had from mine, and I gripped the sides, wondering if our journey would begin with a ducking. But Devlin sat down and the boat glided on into the mist. He slid the oars into the rowlocks, and settled them to his grip before taking the first, smooth stroke.

The blades dipped in and out of the water with hardly a sound. We floated through the tendrils of mist along Devlin's Stretch. Behind us the cottage grew smaller and smaller, until we turned the bend and it was gone. The bush was black and solid either side of us. Devlin caught my eye and spoke to me softly, encouragingly.

'Danny was always a man for the ladies. He'll steal your heart from me, you'll see.'

I smiled back. It was easier than saying what we both knew, that there would never be anyone else for either of us.

'We're near.' He murmured at last the words I dreaded.

I had already smelt the acrid smell of woodsmoke and heard the barks of Cromarty's dogs, muffled through the mist. The barracks were close, it was only a matter of time.

Devlin used one of his oars to turn us towards the shore. The bush was sparser now, where it had been thinned by the need for firewood and building materials. The moon came out. The riverbank looked deserted. If Danny was waiting, he was well hidden.

As we drew closer, we stopped speaking. I could see the shore properly now. The river was running low and its bank was level with the top of my head. There were two wooden poles rising from the water which were used to tie up visiting vessels. I supposed a sturdy plank would be placed across the gap from deck to shore to make unloading easier. The mist curled about us.

Devlin employed his oar to smooth our progress, and we came neatly to rest between the poles and the bank.

We sat still, listening, waiting.

'Perhaps—' I began, but he put up his hand and I stopped. There was a faint chink and the crunch of approaching footsteps. They didn't seem to be trying to be quiet. I heard Barnet's voice, a low mumble. Oddly, it sounded as if he were berating his prisoner.

Two figures appeared on the edge of the bank above us, their faces pale and ghostly. Devlin half rose from his seat, causing the boat to rock dangerously.

'Danny?' he whispered in a strained voice. 'Danny, is it you?'

I saw Barnet, his hand on the other man's arm as if he were restraining him. Indeed, Danny had a length of chain from his wrists to his ankles, fastened there by iron cuffs and looped to his waist on a belt. Evidently Barnet had been unable, or unwilling, to release him, but there were rags wrapped around the chains, as if to muffle the sounds they made. Danny was stooped over like an old man, his head cocked inquiringly to one side as he gazed down at us.

A frisson of terror and dismay lifted the skin on my arms.

'Thomas Devlin,' Danny said, in a voice as rough and splintery as unmilled timber. I saw him smile, though his eyes were dead. I knew him. It was the convict whose face I had looked into at the fire, the one who had called me 'Kate'.

'Danny!' Devlin reached up his hand. 'Come on, now. Come into the boat.'

But Barnet pushed forward, still with that grip on Danny's arm. 'I want me money first,' he reminded us in a belligerent voice. I could smell the rum on him from where I sat.

Devlin paused, taken aback, and then he dug his hand into his pocket. 'You'll have your money.'

Barnet grunted. 'I hope you know what you've bought yourself, Devlin. This one's as mad as they come. They call him Cromarty's dog, 'cause he does Cromarty's bidding ... and the rest!'

He laughed.

I felt Devlin's anger rolling off him in waves, but he said nothing, merely produced the leather purse and tossed it up towards the soldier. Barnet snatched at it and missed. Cursing, he knelt down on the ground to search for it. Free now, Danny stood swaying and staring out over the river.

'Devlin,' I whispered, 'he's not well. Danny's not himself.'

He looked at me strangely, and then loyalty to his friend made him shake his head. 'He'll be all right when we've taken him home. He needs good food and a good fire, and then we'll be away, won't we Danny?'

Danny nodded. 'Away to Dublin Castle,' he agreed.

There was a pause, and then Devlin laughed as if it were a joke, but I sensed his dismay. He must know in his heart it was no joke. 'Danny?' he said softly, gently. Again he held out his hand. There was a moment when I was sure Danny wouldn't take it, and then he grasped Devlin's fingers, and Devlin swung him down into the boat.

The smell of him was overpowering, and I hastily pulled the folds of my cloak over my nose and mouth, trying not to retch. Danny stumbled, hampered by the chains, but Devlin settled him safely enough in the bow. He was a small, slight man compared to Devlin. I saw Devlin's hands linger on his friend's shoulders.

'You're thin,' he said, more to himself. 'Oh, but you're thin, Danny. Never mind, we'll feed you up. And clean you up, by God you need it! Maybe Kate here will comb your hair, as she combs mine.'

Danny nodded, his eyes fastened on Devlin. His mouth curled into a smile that was more a fixed grimace, like a skull which has no choice but to smile.

Cromarty's dogs had been barking spasmodically for some moments but I hadn't taken any notice of them, I'd been so focused on Danny and Devlin. Now the barking increased, and with it came the tuneless bonging of a bell. Almost at the same time the smell of smoke grew stronger.

Barnet swore foully. Devlin was out of the boat, scrambling up the bank and gripping the soldier by the throat. He shook him so hard I thought his numerous teeth would fall out. 'What've you done?' he cried. 'I said to get 'em drunk, not to burn 'em alive!'

Barnet gasped, choking, trying to catch his breath. 'It weren't me ... it weren't me ...'

Behind them Danny laughed.

Devlin released Barnet and turned back to the boat. He stood, staring down at Danny. Danny smiled back at him.

'Hellfire,' he explained in his grating voice, and nodded his head wisely. ''Tis the only way, Thomas. Fire is clean. I freed it, and fed it.'

I saw pain twist Devlin's face, and then he looked at me. 'I have to go and help,' he said. 'I can't let men die in that. Stay here with Danny, and I'll come back for you both. We'll still get him away.'

Barnet blinked at him in amazement. 'You're as mad as him!' he burst out. 'Dunwich is there an' all! Came this evenin' on his pretty horse. He'll have the lot of us strung up for this!'

But Devlin was already gone, running. There was an explosion of fiery sound. I could see the fire plainly now, roaring high up into the sky. The dogs were still barking their monotonous song, and were joined by a chorus of men shouting and horses screaming. Barnet fumbled the money purse into his coat.

'I weren't here,' he said, and then vanished after Devlin, evidently deciding it was safer to return to the barracks.

CHAPTER ELEVEN

I sat, listening to them go, longing to follow but knowing I couldn't. Devlin had entrusted me with something he held very dear. I had to stay with Danny.

12

The sky was turning red above the barracks, the colour of the fire staining the clouds. I stood up in the boat, clinging to a pole, and stared until my eyes hurt. I could see the brilliant glow that was the barracks, and the dark blur of figures running before it, silhouetted in their terror. But I couldn't see Devlin.

Opposite me, Danny was a shadow, silent and unmoving. I glanced at him now and then, but he didn't speak. I couldn't even see if he was looking at me.

We were alone.

Surely, I thought, my being here now, when I had been in the midst of the fire during my other trip into the past, meant that history *could* be changed? And if history could be changed, perhaps there was a chance for me and Devlin after all.

'They won't put out the fire,' Danny said in his grating voice.

I steadied myself against the pole, looking down at him. 'I know.'

He was peering up at me, his head cocked in that odd way, while his shoulders were hunched over.

'Major Dunwich will take control of the situation, but the barracks will burn to the ground,' I went on, unable to stop myself. 'The convicts who try to escape will be retaken.'

'You're a prophet,' he murmured. Suddenly he moved and reached one hand into his jacket, the manacles on his wrists hampering him. The length of chain from wrist to waist, and again from waist to ankle seemed remarkably short. I had read somewhere that shortening the chains made it more uncomfortable for the convict and was a form of punishment.

'You can see my book,' Danny whispered.

'Book?' I shivered, and knew there was something I should remember. But I couldn't. Too much had happened to me and I couldn't think clearly. I couldn't think of anything but Devlin, and what was happening to him.

Danny drew his hand out, and I could see he held a small parcel. Carefully, he unwrapped it from its oilskin covering and stared down at it. I saw the shadow of his smile in the moonlight.

'I'll go and see if Devlin's all right,' I said, hoping Danny would say, Yes, yes, you go! But he said nothing, and I didn't move. I was afraid to.

Danny held out the book with a quick, almost savage gesture. Fingers trembling, I took it. I could feel that the cover was some sort of hide or leather—it felt warm from Danny's body. I bent closer, knowing I wouldn't be able to read it in this poor light, and opened it.

The silence drew on, but I couldn't speak. He was waiting, watching, but I couldn't appease him. I knew this book. It was the one Jim Wallace had shown me a photocopy of in the Leeward Museum. The book which supposedly had belonged to someone at the barracks. Written in blood, and so crazy it had made no sense.

'Why do you write such things?' I whispered.

'I write the truth,' he replied, smiling.

'I have to find Devlin.' And this time I did move, reaching out to the bank with crooked fingers. The boat tipped dangerously. I caught hold of part of a shrub, and moved to step out onto the steep slope running up the bank, but I couldn't seem to pull myself from the boat. My clothing was caught. I peered over my shoulder, still clinging to the bush with my hands, my feet still in the boat.

Danny was holding on to my hem with one hand, and with the other he was trying to ease the boat from its berth between the poles and the bank, easing it back out into the river.

'Water and fire,' he said, nodding. 'Fire and water. They're best. They'll cleanse you, Kate. It'll not take long. Then it's Thomas's turn.' He leaned closer, speaking to me kindly, as if I were a child. 'That's what suffering's for, Kate. Without suffering there's no heaven. That's why Cromarty makes me suffer.'

I squeaked some reply. I saw the gap beneath me widening as the boat began to move. My hands were losing their grip, and soon I would fall into the river. My beautiful cloak, my gift from Devlin, would fill with water and drag me down. 'Danny, please,' I begged him. 'Devlin and I want to help you! You must bring the boat back so that we can help you ...'

'Help me?' he rasped. 'I don't need help. 'Tis you, Kate, who must be cleansed.'

Something white shifted on the river bank above me. I stared up, thinking it might be Devlin come back. A pair of yellow eyes gleamed in the moonlight. The cat! Oh God, the cat! I whimpered, and stretched out a shaky hand towards it. Slowly, crouching low to the ground, it edged towards me.

The boat was moving properly now, and I knew it was only my hold on the bush that was keeping it moored, and only a matter of seconds before I lost my grip. Danny was singing to himself in a strange, rusty voice. The cat stretched out its head towards me, sniffing at my fingers, and then it made a little greeting sound and began to rub against me with its whiskery cheek.

There was a roaring in my ears, and then nothing.

I was lying on the ground with my arms wrapped around a gum tree. I blinked, becoming aware of the many and various sticks and stones pressing into my skin through my clothing. Despite the balmy autumn evening, I was shivering uncontrollably.

The cat was sitting, watching me, in the middle of what appeared to be a narrow track from the river into the bush … The river. I turned carefully and looked behind me. But the water stretched out peacefully, nothing stirring. Danny was gone, left behind in that other time, and no doubt wondering what had happened to me. But then again, Danny, being what he was, had probably taken it all in his stride.

I sat up, brushing myself off. I was still wearing the cloak and the long dress and my kangaroo skin shoes. A faint smell of smoke from someone's stove reached me, and my priorities reasserted themselves with a bang.

'Devlin.' The whispered thought brought me shakily to my feet. Devlin was back there, at the fire, and I was here. He wouldn't know where I was, or what had happened. I had to tell him. I had to see him. I had to get back to him, now.

I spun around, desperately searching for the cat, but it wasn't there. Whimpering, I began to run along the track where I had last seen it, deeper into the bush. It was darker here. Something bounded across my path, crashing into the scrub, but I didn't stop. I ran on wildly, scratching my outstretched arms on branches and twigs. There was something sticky on my face ... blood. The cut stung when I touched it. But I kept running. Somehow, I still believed I would find Devlin ahead. That he would be waiting for me. Blinded by tears, heart thumping, I stumbled on.

I burst out into the clearing. It was completely silent. The moonlight was much stronger here, out of the dense covering of the trees. I could see the tourist board quite plainly on the other side. But not the cat.

I was alone.

It can't end like this! 'Devlin!' the name came out of my lips in a half cry, half sob. I began to run back and forth across the clearing, looking for something, anything. But there was nothing. Devlin was here, and I was here, but a huge, unbridgeable gap in time separated us.

I tripped on my skirt, and it didn't seem to matter if I saved myself or not. So I let myself go, falling heavily to the ground, and lay there, my face against the earth and the dead leaves. Defeated.

I don't know how much time passed. My hopelessness swamped me and I wallowed in it. But gradually I became aware of a sensation of being watched. Slowly, carefully, I turned my head and met a pair of yellow eyes.

'Oh, *cat*!' I said, and laughed.

It seemed to smile back at me. Didn't mean it, it seemed to say. Just a joke. I watched it stretch and stroll towards me until it was close enough, and then I reached out and drew it into my arms.

It was like Danny's hellfire.

Flames rose with a roaring sound close beside me. The heat singed my eyebrows. I gasped for air, shielding my face. Ashes and cinders floated about me, while men ran and screamed. Some timbers fell crashing into the fire and it was as if someone had opened the door into a furnace. The moisture was baked from my skin.

Someone took my arm, pulling at me, and I cried out. I was back in 1829 and we had shot this scene before—only my costume was different. Sure enough, there was the little hut, full of supplies for the convicts, and there—I spun around, wild-eyed—*there* was Major Dunwich.

He was glaring at me from his soot-blackened face. His lips were moving, and I read them: 'What are you doing here?' It was the same man, exactly. I gawked at him.

'I asked you what you are doing here?' he demanded in a voice like a headmaster.

'I'm on holiday,' I heard myself say, and flinched.

He gave me a glare as hot as the fire, and then walked off, his voice booming above the noise. 'Get that water over here! Now, you whoreson!'

I groaned and covered my face with my hands. No, it couldn't be, it couldn't be happening again. Things could be changed, couldn't they? I had pinned all my hopes on the theory that history could be changed, and now I was being proved wrong.

There was a violent bump against my shoulder. My flesh crept with a new terror. Slowly I lifted my head, knowing what I would see and realising I had no choice.

Danny was standing there.

Some cool part of my brain noticed that he had rid himself of his chains. He must have hurt himself, too, because his foot was cut and bleeding. I wondered how he had got out of the boat and back to the barracks. I wondered why he had come. And all the time I was wondering, I was looking into his face. This was Danny, I told myself, the boy Devlin had grown up with and loved. Danny, who had taken Devlin's pain away with the healing power of his hands, and thus enabled Devlin to do the same for me. I must help him!

'Where's Devlin?' I asked him, my lips stiff and hard to manage.

There was nothing remotely human in him, I

realised sadly. Those eyes were as empty as space. It was useless pretending he could be reached. 'You'll come with me now, Kate.' He said it as if it were a quite rational suggestion.

The heat of the fire was roasting my back, but I was cold. I shook my head.

And then to my relief, Major Dunwich made his reappearance, his sergeant major's voice roaring out behind me. 'Get on to the bucket brigade! Move, you whoreson!'

Danny looked past me, and I saw a shadow of uncertainty or cunning cross his face, and then he ducked his head and ran away into the billowing clouds of smoke. I watched to make sure he was really gone.

Dunwich was still shouting at the men. The barracks were burning fiercely now, bits falling off in all directions. The smoke and debris were so thick, I had to cover the lower half of my face with my cloak to breathe. More of the roof caved in, creating a big gap in the middle of the building. I found I was looking right through to the other side. And there was Devlin.

Last time I had seen only a shadow, but I saw more this time. I saw him and he saw me. He was half supporting another man, and he'd stripped down to his shirt and trousers. I saw the blank look on his soot streaked face as he realised I was here, in the midst of chaos, instead of where I was supposed to be, back in the boat with Danny. In that moment, nothing else mattered but being with Devlin.

'Devlin!' I screamed, running forward. 'Devlin!'

But I'd forgotten my friend, Major Dunwich. 'Get back! It's not safe.' He placed himself in front of me like some sort of policeman with a riot shield, and I cannoned into him. I gave a cry of frustrated pain and anger, and tried to slip around him. But he caught my arm and gave it a nasty squeeze, holding me captive. Beyond us, the fire was far from anyone's control.

'What a waste,' Dunwich said. 'Someone will have to pay for this, eh, Cromarty!'

Edging closer to Dunwich, I peered around, and there he was, the evil overseer, materialising from the billowing smoke.

'Aye, sir,' he grovelled. 'We'll have the truth out of 'em all right, sir.'

'Well, *you* will,' I muttered.

'The governor will want a detailed report. He's most particular when it comes to detail. It wouldn't surprise me if he inspects the damage himself.' The major was saying his lines. I kept my eyes on Cromarty; he was the one to watch.

He was nodding, but I knew him better now. I saw the contempt in his eyes, gleaming within their fleshy folds.

'I want you to see to it, Cromarty.'

'Aye, I will sir, don't you worry none, sir, it'll be dealt with, sir.'

'You toad,' I said. It seemed appropriate to both the era and the man.

They looked at me, the Major with a sort of

surprised curiosity and Cromarty with pleased malevolence.

'What are you doing here?' Dunwich asked. 'You were calling for Devlin. Are you this Devlin's wife?'

Cromarty dived in for his revenge. 'Devlin in't got a wife, Major. This is his woman, sir.'

I glared back at him.

'She's been livin' over at his cottage, sir.' Major Dunwich gave me the 'fallen woman' look. 'Indeed. What is your name, madam?'

'My name is Kate O'Hara,' I said loudly. 'And this man is mistreating the men in his care,' and I pointed at Cromarty, so that there would be no mistaking whom I meant. 'I suggest you question a few of them and see what they have to say—'

Cromarty growled like one of his dogs and grabbed my arm, but he got no further. The poor man with the cut cheek was panting up behind us with his news. 'They're out, sir! They've bolted!'

Cromarty and Dunwich turned as one. 'How many?' boomed the Major.

'About half a dozen, sir,' was the man's answer.

'Ten, actually,' I murmured, rubbing my bruised arm.

But they were no longer interested in me. 'Check on the weapons!' Dunwich instructed, and they were off, into the maelstrom.

I was tempted to set off after them and search for Devlin, but I was afraid of Cromarty. There had been murder in his eyes just now and if he found me alone, he might just decide to barbecue me.

I began to step unobtrusively backwards, towards the edge of the bush, and then stopped, remembering what had happened last time, when the cat had brushed my ankle. I'd made that frantic journey once tonight, and once was enough. I had to stay and find Devlin. I had to stick to him like glue.

This was the night he disappeared without trace.

13

I moved cautiously around the perimeter of the clearing, towards the side where I had seen Devlin. Everyone seemed far too busy to notice me, but I wanted to be sure. One of Cromarty's dogs ran up to me, snuffling at my skirts, and then turned and ran off again.

Major Dunwich was standing in a circle of soldiers and guards, with a large group of convicts seated on the ground to one side. Most of them had had their chains removed, and I supposed this was done when the fire started.

They looked on, faces lit by the flames, as grimy as their gaolers.

And then I saw Devlin. He was standing closer to the fire, shading his eyes against the heat of the furnace that had once been the convict barracks. He looked blackened and exhausted. I had started towards him before I realised he was bending his head to speak to someone half obscured beside him.

It was Cromarty.

He was pointing, back towards the river. I saw Devlin lift his head and nod. And then Major Dunwich and his gang began to split up, some remaining to guard the convicts on the ground, the rest heading into the bush in various directions. Major Dunwich was doing a lot of what he did best—shouting. As he strode past Devlin and Cromarty he stopped and had a word with them.

The three men spoke briefly, and then Devlin and Cromarty turned and moved into the trees, following the track towards the river ... and the boat. Dunwich watched them a moment, and then began to shout more orders.

Something in me tightened. I didn't like that Devlin had gone with Cromarty. I didn't like this turn of events at all. I didn't like Cromarty. Whirling my cloak about me like a Brontë heroine, I set off after them.

'Ma'am!' Dunwich, damn him. 'You must stay here with us until the prisoners are under guard again!'

I waved my hand at him with a smile, and kept walking. 'I'm with Devlin!' I called.

'Devlin asked that I protect you, ma'am! Come back!'

I didn't stop. My back was twitching with the thought that any moment Dunwich would grab me, but when I finally gave in to the urge to glance back, he was still with his men, though the look he was sending after me was full of venom.

I was back in the bush, on practically the same track I had run down moments before ... in the future. It had been quieter then. Now all about me I could hear the crashing of men through the trees and the calling of the guards and soldiers as they searched for the escapees. I moved slowly, carefully, listening. As I went, I seemed to leave most of the searchers behind. I wasn't in the position of having to examine every bush and could move more quickly. Far behind me, the fire crackled and smouldered. Smoke and ash drifted down over the area and over me. I pulled my cloak closer about me, snuggling into its warmth.

The burning of the convict barracks had been a major catastrophe. I wondered why I hadn't told Dunwich that Danny had started it when I had the chance, but somehow I hadn't been able to get the words out. I already knew that Danny would be recaptured—they would all be recaptured. Surely that was punishment enough for him. I was more concerned with Devlin.

I could hear the river now, moving against its banks. The bushland on the other side was dark and silent, and the blue velvet sky above streaked with clouds. The moon was setting, hanging over the trees like a scythe. Gradually, I became aware of footsteps ahead of me, and voices. One of them was Devlin's.

The voices were getting louder. Devlin and his companion had stopped. A soldier crashed through the bush beside me. I moved closer to the trunk of a tree, pressing myself against it and pulling my cloak around my face. He passed by without seeing me, veering off downstream. The place was chaos, just as I had imagined.

'... not here.'

Devlin was speaking, but I couldn't quite hear him. I began to move, choosing each step with great deliberation. The boat nosed against the riverbank with a bumping noise. Danny must have brought it back to shore after my timely escape. The thought of Danny made my flesh creep. Where was he now?

As if in answer to my silent question, I heard Cromarty say, 'Danny came back to me.'

Devlin didn't reply; I held my breath.

'Do you think he wouldn't have told me what you were plannin'?' Cromarty went on softly, contemptuously. 'He wouldn't leave me, he can't. He's my creature now.' And he laughed in a way that made my blood run hot.

I didn't hear what Devlin said next, I was too angry, but Cromarty replied with, 'He weeps in me arms like a girl. He tells me all about you, Devlin. Sometimes, he even pretends I am you.'

I flinched. Devlin would find such a thing as appalling as I did. I listened, heart pounding, as Devlin quietly said, 'I'm going to cut your balls off, and watch you eat them.'

Cromarty laughed. 'You're a brave man, are you, Devlin?' There was a savagery in his voice that scared me. Hell hath no fury, I thought, like an overseer scorned.

I was close enough now to see them, standing on the riverbank, two large silhouettes. Cromarty glanced behind him, and for a moment I thought he had caught sight of me in the trees, but then he said, quite gently, 'Danny? Come here, Danny.'

A figure moved only a few steps in front of me—if I had crept any closer, I would have bumped into him. I watched, frozen, as he went to join the other two. It *was* Danny. He stood in that peculiar hunched way beside his master. Cromarty reached down and put his arm around the smaller man's shoulders.

'Danny, here's Devlin. Devlin don't like us, Danny. He don't like me. What are you goin' to do about it, Danny?'

Danny cocked his head, watching Devlin in that sideways way he had. 'He doesn't like us?' he asked, smiling.

'No, he don't like us. What should we do, Danny? What did we do last time someone didn't like us, eh? What did we do, Danny?' His voice was full of suppressed excitement.

'We cleansed him,' Danny replied.

'That's it. That's it.' Cromarty was just about jumping up and down. 'We have to show him, don't we? We have to make him sorry. So we'll cleanse him in the river, Danny.'

I saw Devlin shake his head, as if he couldn't believe what he was hearing. 'Danny,' he whispered, 'I'll get you away, somewhere where you don't have to ... away from this pig of a man. Do you hear me, old friend?' He put his hand out gently, as if to touch him.

But Danny didn't hear him. He hadn't heard anyone but Cromarty in a long time. I moved as if to step out and take Devlin's side. But something stopped me, keeping me frozen still amongst the trees. My arm wrapped around the harsh bark of a small tree, and the peppermint scent of it filled my head. Further along the river, the curlews gave their mournful, warning cry, and then a gunshot sounded, echoing down the valley.

Cromarty lifted his head with a pleased grunt. 'Some whoreson's had his liberty cut short!' he said, in a mockery of Dunwich's educated tones. 'You're wastin' your time with Danny, you know, boatman. Danny don't want his liberty. Do you, Danny? He's happy here with me. I have work for him.'

Danny stared at him intently, as if Cromarty were speaking a language he finally understood.

'Danny,' Devlin said sharply, and reluctantly the smaller man turned to face him. 'Remember Dublin Castle, Danny,' he went on, in a voice at once gentle and harsh. 'Remember the men marchin', Danny, and the colour of their blood. Remember the gaol, and my head hurting so that I begged you to kill me. But you didn't. You had the healing touch, Danny. Don't waste it on this pig of a man.'

But Danny didn't answer, and then Cromarty was urging, 'Come on Danny, you'd best get to it!' He rubbed his hands together in anticipation. 'Let's see him to the pearly gates, before I freeze.'

Danny reached out and grasped Devlin's upper arms. Devlin looked down at him, his face twisted with sadness and disgust. 'You won't do what this pig tells you to, will you, Danny?' he asked, bending his head so that he could peer down into his friend's eyes. 'Danny, we played together before we took our first steps. We mean more to each other than this piece of shite.'

Cromarty laughed silently. I knew then what it was all about. Cromarty felt slighted by Devlin, and he wanted to punish him, and the best way of punishing him was using Danny to do it for him. How many other times had he done the same thing? The question was unanswerable and horrifying.

'Oh Danny,' he said now, 'you won't listen to him, will you? I wouldn't like it, would I?'

Danny hesitated. Perhaps the past did reside there, somewhere in his empty mind, but it was too far away and too faded to account for much. He braced himself, pushing Devlin towards the bank and the river.

He must have been stronger than he looked, or perhaps Devlin was unprepared, for he stumbled and had to take several steps back to regain his balance. Then he set his hands to Danny's shoulders, pushing back at him. Cromarty edged forward, urging his protégé on. The excitement in his voice was as frightening in its way as Danny's emptiness.

Devlin was obviously trying his best not to hurt Danny, using minimal force. Was that what Cromarty wanted? For the two men who had once been so close to fight to the death? Did he get some sort of satisfaction from that? Danny would fight but Devlin was trying very hard not to fight at all. If it came to a final, desperate choice, would Devlin be able to kill Danny to save himself?

I had to do something, before it came to that. I couldn't risk losing Devlin now; he was more important than my fear of Cromarty and Danny. On shaky legs, I slipped around behind them, slinking closer to the riverbank. The boat was moored where it had been before, nosing the bank as the swell lifted it gently up and down. I dropped onto my bottom and half slid and half wriggled down the steep slope towards it, quick as I could. A small avalanche of earth and leaves preceded me. My feet touched wood, the boat tilted. I hesitated, preparing myself to make the final leap to safety.

'Bitch.'

Cromarty had seen me. I stared into his eyes a

second too long, and then he had moved, so quickly I had no chance, and grabbed me.

I screamed.

Devlin had been so busy with Danny, he hadn't noticed anything else. The sound of my scream brought his head up. Danny chose that moment to strike hard, lurching against him. They both teetered briefly on the riverbank, and then fell backwards into the dark water. I heard the splash, and saw them surface, arms still clasped about each other.

Cromarty was on his knees, stretching forward to haul me in by my cloak. I was kicking and gasping like a fish about to be landed. There was more splashing where Devlin and Danny had gone in, but Cromarty didn't seem concerned with them. Terrified, I glanced back and saw the light in his little piggy eyes. He wanted me.

His grip on my cloak tightened. I felt him dragging me inexorably closer. God, he was strong—my feet were making a groove in the earth as I dug my heels in. 'Let me go!' I shrieked, angry and scared, all at once. Cromarty liked that. He laughed and gave my cloak another jerk, making me lose my grip. I screamed, rolling to one side, but he dragged me back. Take off the cloak, I thought. I began to fumble desperately with the fastenings. If I could take it off, I could get away.

My fingers were numb with cold and shock. I whimpered, tearing a nail. I had long ago

stopped being aware of Devlin or Danny, or anyone but Cromarty and me.

The fastenings wouldn't come undone.

I looked behind me and saw Cromarty's
smile. He was enjoying himself, toying with me.
He could have captured me in the first few
moments if he'd really wanted to.

'Come on,' he said. 'Bitch.'

The hatred in his eyes wasn't just for me, but
for all humankind.

I dug my heels into the ground again, and
with a mighty effort pulled against his grip. He
lost it and I slid frantically down toward the boat.
But he slithered after me. I heard his grunt of
triumph as his fingers tangled in my cloak again,
and brought me up short.

'Enough,' he said coldly. 'I'll have you now.'

I turned, white-faced, and froze. Devlin,
sopping wet, hair and clothes clinging to him,
was moving up behind us. As I watched, open
mouthed, he raised his boot and gave Cromarty a
savage, well-aimed kick.

Cromarty went catapulting forward, into the
river.

There was a great splash, and then he surfaced, floundering and gasping for air. I wondered if he could swim. I hoped not.

Free now, I finished my slide into the boat
and climbed in, twisting to look up at Devlin.
He hesitated, half turning as if to go back, and
then there was a crashing of men coming through
the trees. Devlin made his decision, leaping into

the boat. It rocked wildly. He grabbed up the oars and pushed off just as Cromarty paddled towards it. We were moving away, out into the river.

'Bolter! Bolter!' Cromarty was screaming, hair plastered to his head.

Devlin was rowing furiously, each stroke so powerful we were propelled arrow-like into the middle of the dark river. 'Danny?' I asked him, trying to catch my breath.

He didn't stop rowing. 'I held him under. I had to,' he gasped. 'He was trying to kill me.'

'But ...' I peered forward at him, trying to see his face in the darkness. 'Is he dead?' I whispered, sorrow filling me. But the sorrow was for Devlin, not Danny.

Devlin shook his head.

There were more shouts back on the river-bank. I turned to look, and my eyes were momentarily caught and held by the red glow of the fire, like an early sunrise, through the trees. Cromarty was out of the water, looking like a clothed hippopotamus. 'Shoot him!' he was yelling, beside himself. He was dancing about, his wet clothing flapping.

There was a red flash, and something went past me, coal hot, and struck the river.

'They're shooting at us,' I said in disbelief. 'Devlin, they're shooting at us!'

'So they are,' he replied grimly, and kept rowing. We were well out into the river now, and the next red flash I saw fell short of us. Soon, we would be out of sight. Soon, we would be back in Devlin's Stretch.

He stopped.

I looked at him uncertainly. 'Devlin? Are you ... God, are you hurt?' Frantically, I searched over him with shaking hands. His clothing was wet from his dunking in the water, but he seemed whole. 'Devlin?'

He caught my fingers tight in his. 'I have to go back for Danny.'

I stared at him as if he were mad, as mad as Danny and Cromarty. I shook his hands off mine. 'No.'

'He's alive. Kate ... he knows me. He's waiting for me. There was a half-rotten log a few yards from where we went in, it's stuck in the bank there. I left him by it in the water and hanging on. I said, "Stay here, Danny, I'll come for you," and he lay still as a lamb, and looked up at me and said, "I'm thinking of the old days, Thomas. Don't worry for me any more, I'll be waiting." And it was him, it was Danny.' He gave me a melancholy look. 'I can't leave him.'

I knew he couldn't, but still I argued. I had my happiness to consider. 'Cromarty will kill you if you go back. He won't harm Danny, you heard what Barnet said.'

'How can you say that?' he whispered. 'How can you, when you know ... you know ...' He couldn't go on, and neither could I. Devlin's loyalty to Danny was admirable; Danny had saved his life, and now Devlin must return the favour. But I was very much afraid I would never see him again.

'I know you have to go,' I said quietly, 'but I wish you didn't.'

He reached forward and pulled me into his arms. There were tears on my face that I didn't remember crying. 'I'm going into the river now, sweet Kate,' he murmured. 'I'll swim back to where I left him. I'll take care. When I have Danny, I'll bring him back to the boat. Wait here until dawn, and if I haven't come by then, row on to the cottage.'

'And then?' I whispered. 'What then?'

'I'll come to you, Kate, the river will bring me.'

My skin went icy. Was this where it ended? Where it had begun? With the river. I held him a moment longer, trying to remember the feel of him. And then he put me away and the boat rocked as he climbed across to the side. He pulled off his boots and jacket, and laid them in the bottom of the boat. There was a gentle splash as he slipped over the side and into the river. His face turned up to me, a pale oval in the darkness.

'Devlin,' I whispered, 'Devlin.' I couldn't think of anything else to say.

'Wait for me,' he whispered back. 'Do you promise? Wait for me, Kate.'

'I'll wait,' I promised.

He was gone, swimming so quietly I hardly

heard him, and after a moment I couldn't see him either.

'Devlin?' I whispered, but he didn't answer. The boat rocked gently. A soft breeze brushed my hair, and I felt the damp mist against my cheek, like a dead man's kiss, drifting down Devlin's Stretch.

14

I waited. I waited until the dawn began to lighten the steely sky and the glow of the fire faded into a grey pall of smoke. But Devlin did not return.

I began to row, slowly, awkwardly, towards the cottage.

It took me a long time to find the rhythm that Devlin had. At first I was so chilled from sitting out in the cold for so long, I had difficulty with any movement, and then my arms and back began to ache. But I welcomed the pain. It stopped me thinking of Devlin.

The cottage looked deserted. I waited a moment, searching the area with care before I rowed the final few metres to the bank. Once there, I struggled to drag the boat far enough up onto the bank to secure it. My arms were like lead now, and the hems of my skirt and cloak were wet and clinging to my legs.

I sank down onto the ground and put my head in my hands. I wanted to grieve. He was gone, and with all my knowledge of the future I hadn't been able to do a thing about it.

'Where's the boatman?'

The question brought my head up and around. Howard Tuck gave the white-faced, wild-eyed creature before him an uncertain look. He looked scruffy, his hair standing on end, and there was a smear of soot on one cheek. I suspected Howard had been hiding, watching the antics at the convict barracks.

'The boatman, Devlin,' Howard repeated, looking brave and apprehensive at the same time. 'He said he was going to give me a ride in his boat.'

Hope stirred in me, and I clambered to my feet, impatiently pulling the wet skirt out of the way. 'Have you seen him?'

Howard frowned. 'Only at the fire. He was helping put it out.'

'But afterwards … have you seen him since?'

Howard shook his head. 'There's nothing happening there now. The Major has them

building a sort of shelter for tonight, and he's
sent someone off to tell the Governor. I heard him
saying my Ma has to supply some of our sheep for
meat. She'll be pleased. She'll make 'em pay.'

I walked past him, towards the cottage.
Perhaps Devlin was inside, I thought, but I knew
it was empty. It looked empty. It felt empty.
Inside, the fire was cold. I stood in the bedroom
and noted the depression in the bed where Devlin
and I had lain. Tears burned in my eyes, threatening to overflow. Howard shuffled uneasily behind
me, sensing a possible scene.

'I could go back and have a look,' he
suggested uncertainly.

I glanced around at him. He was right.
Someone had to go back and look. I knew I
should tell Howard to go home, that I would
handle it, but I needed company, even the company of an eight-year-old boy. Besides, I doubted
Howard would let me go alone anyway. He had
the light of adventure in his eye.

'We'll both go,' I said at last. 'But you'll stay
close to me, OK?'

He blinked. 'Oh ... what? Oh Kate?'

'Never mind,' I muttered, and went into the
other room. There was some of Devlin's coarse,
dry bread on the table and I took a lump and
began to chew it. Howard's stomach rumbled
loudly beside me, and I broke off a bigger piece
for him. He ate like a ravenous little animal, and
I eyed him with a stirring of amusement.

'Won't your mother be worrying about you?'

I asked him curiously, as I poured us both water from the jug.

Howard looked at me with limpid eyes, behind which lurked cunning. 'Ma? No, she won't worry.'

I nodded as if I believed him, and looked about. Everything was as Devlin had left it. The trunk was there, closed, waiting for his journey south with Danny. I went over and touched it lightly. I traced his name. In a moment I really would start to cry.

'We'll go now,' I said briskly, turning back to Howard. 'Are you ready?'

He nodded enthusiastically, cramming the rest of the bread into his mouth.

We set off into the chilly dawn light, down the track through the bush to the convict barracks, me first, my wet skirts dragging through the leaves, Howard trotting behind me.

I could smell the smoke even this far from the fire. Would they have heard of it in Leeward yet? I expected that Major Dunwich would have everything under control. Had Danny been recaptured? And Devlin with him? Was that why he hadn't returned? Or had Danny slunk back to Cromarty and the two of them finished what they had begun? I shivered, rubbing at my arms. It was no use speculating. I must keep a clear and cool head.

I saw Dunwich's red coat long before he saw me. He was coming towards me on foot, a couple of soldiers trailing after him. They looked as if they hadn't slept all night, and certainly hadn't had a wash or change of clothing.

The Major caught sight of me at last. He looked older in the daylight; his expression wasn't very welcoming either. 'Madam!' he boomed. The two men behind him glanced at me with dark-circled, weary eyes. As the Major drew to a halt before me, they took the opportunity to lean on their guns.

'Major Dunwich,' I said, in my strongest voice. 'I'm looking for Devlin.'

Something flicked across his tired face, and I recognised it as puzzlement. 'Devlin, the boatman? He was with us last night. A very courageous man. Yes, I won't stint my praise to the Governor when I speak of Devlin! But he isn't here now. Cromarty said he went home. There was some kerfuffle by the river after he'd gone. One of the convicts tried to swim out into the river and was fired upon. He drowned, poor devil.'

I swallowed carefully. 'Who drowned?'

'It was Danny O'Brien. One of the worst, it seems. There wasn't a mark on him. He must have thought he could reach the other side of the river, weakened, tried to swim back, and was drowned. It was very cold.'

'Yes,' I said, oddly calm. 'It was very cold.'

Danny had drowned. Had Devlin found him again and tried to swim with him to the boat? Then where was Devlin? If Danny was drowned, had Devlin drowned too, trying to save him? Oh Devlin ...

I didn't think I spoke aloud, but I must have. 'Madam?' Dunwich took my arm in his. I realised I was shaking so much I could hardly stand. The Major gave Howard a hard look. 'Here, boy! Take her back home. She needs to rest. A little rum, perhaps, eh! I'll see what can be done about Devlin. He'll be nearby somewhere.'

I nodded, and allowed Howard to take my hand in his warm, sticky fingers. I don't remember him leading me back to the cottage, but the next moment he was relighting the fire and glancing over his shoulder at me, an uncertain look on his face. He probably judged women by his angry mother; at any moment they could erupt into bad temper.

I put a hand to my eyes. 'You'd better go home now,' I said evenly. 'Your mother will be worried and ... it's safer if you go.' I took my hand away and gave him a long, serious look. 'Do you know the overseer, Cromarty?'

Howard nodded, his eyes as big as plums.

'He's an evil man, a dangerous man. You mustn't ever go near him, Howard, ever.'

'I won't.'

'Good.' I nodded, suddenly very, very tired. 'Good. I'll wait here for Devlin to come.'

'Will he come?' Howard asked quietly.

'He promised,' I murmured, my eyes closing. I couldn't seem to keep them open. 'Thank you, Howard. Now go home.'

The last thing I was aware of was Howard's

breath on my cheek, as he hovered over me, and said in a slow, serious voice, 'Oh Kate.'

I drifted in and out of sleep as the long day drew on. Alone in the cottage, with nothing to interrupt, my thoughts were my companions. Some were welcome—Devlin, Howard. Some were unwelcome—Cromarty and Danny ... Why had no record remained of Danny's death? Was he of so little importance? Or had official-dom muffled the truth for fear of criticism? Poor Danny. I could only hope he had found an afterlife less fearsome than the one he believed in.

As darkness filled the room, I stirred the fire, and waited. And waited still, as a new dawn stole through the shutters, a few milky threads of sunlight venturing out, the vanguard of another long, winter's day.

Devlin had not returned.

There was an emptiness in me that nothing could fill. There was no hope left. Danny was drowned and dead, and so must Devlin be. They had been together, and Danny's body had been found while Devlin's had been taken away, into the depths of the river. It had been, as Major Dunwich said, very cold.

Wait for me. I'll come back.

The memory of his words echoed about me. Devlin had kept his promise, kept it in the only way a dead man could. His ghost had come back to me in the darkness of the night, rowing to shore as he had in life. He had returned to his cottage and to me. I had wanted to know what Devlin's ghost sought, and now I did. He loved me still.

It gave me no comfort.

I went to the window and stared out at the river, like a silver ribbon in the dawn. The boat was gone. A shiver went through me, but I knew Devlin hadn't taken it. He would never have gone without me. Perhaps Howard had taken it; he'd said he wanted a ride in it. But more likely I had failed to secure it properly and it had drifted away. That seemed appropriate, somehow. The river had taken both boat and boatman.

Something stirred near the hearth, and I turned. The white cat sat there, a blob of brilliance in a room turning from grey. 'What will we do now, cat?' I asked it softly. 'How will we manage without him?'

It made a soft, chirruping noise, and started towards me. Like Cleopatra and the asp, I put out my hand and waited for its touch.

I slept all morning; I had had little enough the previous night. When I finally woke, stumbling groggily out into the afternoon sunlight, I found that my painting gear was still there, sitting on the verandah. The sketchbook was a soggy mess, but the rest was all right. I dried off what I could, automatically, not knowing what else to do. I felt light-headed. Perhaps all this time travelling wasn't good for me. Perhaps it had side effects no-one had ever suspected. But I knew my light-headedness was more likely from lack of food.

I sat down on the chair and stared at nothing. I had seen the past, but it was like a tiny piece from a large cake. Like reading one chapter from a book of twenty chapters. What had happened next? I wanted to know. I needed to know. I wanted to slot every fact neatly into place.

'What does it matter?' I asked aloud. 'He's dead.'

Grief swamped me, but a stubborn niggling doubt refused to be submerged. No-one had ever found the body. Usually there was a body. Even if one drowned in the river, a body would turn up, eventually. Look at Danny! And Dunwich would have been searching for Devlin; if he was to be found, Dunwich would have found him. There had been rumours, according to the older Howard, but nothing more. And Howard had refused to tell what he knew.

If indeed he knew anything!

Perhaps there was something I had missed? I forced myself to stand up and go inside the cottage and find Howard's book. It was by the bed. I sat down and looked at it, then I turned it over and looked at the face on the back. Yes, I could see Howard in this old man's face. They were the same eyes, with their bravado and vulnerability, but grown more sure of themselves.

I opened the book and found the bits
concerning the fire. It was as I remembered.
Devlin had disappeared and rumour was rife, but
nothing made much sense. Here was Howard's
infuriating statement: *'As to the truth of the matter,
that is something Devlin wanted to remain a mystery,
and I have kept my promise to leave it so.'*

What had Howard known? I shook my head,
automatically reading on. Here were details of
Howard's visit to his uncle, later his benefactor,
the shipbuilder. His father, it appeared, had died
by this time—it was one year later, 1830. I felt
frustrated and angry. The answer was here
somewhere, I knew it, if only I could find it!

I tossed the book aside. It fell open at the
front endpapers. There was an inscription I
hadn't noticed before. I reached out to pull it
closer, tilting my head to read it. My finger
trembled as I traced the words.

*'I dedicate this book to my Uncle Thomas, boat
builder of Half Moon Bay, and his wife, Kate.'*

Everything inside me stopped, then started
again with a roaring rush. It must be, it had to
be. Half Moon Bay, where Devlin had sailed a
cutter and almost died in a storm. *My Uncle
Thomas and his wife Kate.* Was this it? Was this
the answer?

Outside something began to stir. The air
rippled across the water, and shadows chased each
other from shore to shore. There was a storm
coming. I listened, unmoving. I felt the cottage
stirring about me, like something waking from a

long sleep. 'Devlin?' I murmured, my voice lifted in hope and trepidation. There was a distant rumble of thunder.

The darkness descended quickly. Clouds like dirty finger smudges lined the horizon, and with them came a cold, sharp wind. The river moved restlessly.

I lit candles in every room, as if to light his way. I put on the musk-scented dress and the fur-lined cloak. I knew if I stopped to think the doubts would destroy the hope I had built for myself since I read the dedication in Howard's book. I had even fetched a map from the car, and looked up Half Moon Bay on it. A tiny inlet, curved and secret, south of Hobart.

Above the mantelpiece, the painting grew darker with the loss of light. The boatman and his passenger rowed silently on the moonlit river. I felt more regret at leaving the painting than I did at leaving anything else. I would miss it more than the life I had led with Ian. I felt as far removed from the woman who had been Kate O'Hara as it was possible to be.

As I sat and waited, I read what Howard wrote of his uncle with new eyes. Thomas hadn't been a blood relative, he had been a friend. When Howard's father died, Thomas had taken the boy through a fondness for him and brought him up. Thomas had begun his trade in a small way and gradually built it up into a thriving business. He had died, if not a wealthy man, then certainly a satisfied one. And Kate? Kate had been there, and although Howard didn't say a great deal about her, I could tell he had loved her. He called her, 'Oh Kate.' It was a joke between them.

Oh Kate ... The flesh on my arms prickled.

The wind was gusting through the gum tree and rattling the guttering. The river slapped the shore. I went to the window and peered out. The cat sat near the jetty and, with a trembling indrawn breath, I followed the direction of its gaze. Was there a shadow on the water? It was dark, but the darkness had a strange greenish tinge. *Was* there a shadow?

My hands were wet with perspiration and I wiped them on my skirts. My eyes were aching with the strain of staring out into the gloom. A splattering of rain came across the water, churning it up and closing me in. As it cleared, I saw the boatman.

He was moving through the water with a sure, steady stroke. The bow cut the turbulence like an arrow aiming at the shore, and the cottage. And me. *Devlin*. I felt the word form on my lips, but no sound came. A great wave of longing arose in me, swamping any fears or regrets.

I ran down the passage to the front door. My hands were still slippery, and I had trouble with the knob. I had to use part of my cloak to turn it. The wind took the door and crashed it back against the wall. My hair and skirts whipped about me. Another gust came, and cold rain stung my eyes so that I could hardly see. I stepped forward uncertainly, out onto the uneven bricks, and peered into the wild night. The boat was closer, slicing through the choppy waves. I could see the swing of the oars.

'Devlin!' I cried, and the storm carried my words away. He had come for me! I was running down the riverbank, my cloak flapping about me, the cold stinging my lips and cheeks. At my cry he had turned his head. He was like a shadow, something one can see but never really touch.

The phantom bow of the boat glided forward and struck the bank. Devlin stood up, grey as mist, and I could see the river through him. He was like a photograph that's been superimposed upon another. Insubstantial. A ghost.

But he wasn't alone. Howard was there, a grin splitting his face from ear to ear. I could see his mouth moving as he spoke, but I couldn't hear him. About me the storm howled. My hair whipped across my face, stinging and blinding me. When I pushed it away again, I saw that Devlin was leaning forward, his face level with mine. His eyes gleamed. He stretched out his hand towards me, and I saw his lips silently move. One word. Kate.

The wind screamed across the water. The trees thrashed wildly, lightning stabbed the earth. Out of the corner of my eye I saw something white, crouching defiantly by the jetty.

As I gave Devlin my hand, the white cat made a desperate leap into the boat.

The quiet was as shocking as the chaos of seconds before. The storm had quite simply gone. The sky was dark velvet, full of stars, and not a single cloud marred its perfection. A curlew called out sadly as the boat rocked gently on the calm river. And Devlin's hand in mine was warm and strong and real.

As if someone had suddenly made some celestial adjustment, Howard's voice burst into life. 'He was there, Kate! He was lying on the riverbank. He'd nearly drowned, looking for his friend, and he'd drifted a long way in the cold water. I found him for you, Kate, I found him!'

'Oh you did,' I said, tears filling my eyes. 'You did, Howard.'

Devlin pulled me into his arms, and I felt his heart beating against my cheek. 'I was drownin', Kate, and I dreamed you'd gone far away. I couldn't find you.' His deep voice was shaking. 'The cottage was empty and the world had changed, and though I looked and looked, I couldn't find you.'

'But you did find me,' I whispered. 'We found each other.'

His arms tightened. 'At last.'

Epilogue

The big storm had come down the river valley like an enraged bull, uprooting trees and destroying property. Leeward, too, had suffered. Houses unroofed, electricity lines down and one of the big street trees had crashed through the wall of the Leeward Museum, but luckily no-one was hurt. In fact, only one person had been affected by the entire storm.

And that was Kate O'Hara.

The news was quick to spread—as tragic news always is. Kate O'Hara's friends had arrived from Hobart to visit her and found the cottage empty, though still standing. But Kate was gone.

The police and the people of Leeward searched the countryside around the cottage for days, and the police scuba divers searched the river. They said it was cold and fast-flowing, and if Kate had fallen into the icy water, her body would have been taken far, far downstream. Someone recalled that there had been another disappearance in the river, many years ago— Devlin, a boatman who lived in the cottage. *He* had never been found.

'She must have had one of her headaches,' Dixie said, wiping her eyes and smearing her carefully applied mascara. 'Perhaps the storm confused her, and she wandered away and ... and ... well!' She drew a deep breath and shook her head, not wanting to state the obvious.

Cecil patted her shoulder gently. 'She missed Ian. Perhaps she couldn't go on without him. Perhaps she had been planning it, Dixie.'

'We shouldn't have rushed off that day we came to see her,' Dixie sighed.

Cecil glanced at her, but kindly did not remind her of the circumstances of their hasty leaving.

'I thought ...' Dixie mopped her eyes thoughtfully. 'I thought there was someone staying with her. A man. He was on the river, rowing around in a boat. A big man, with dark hair, and God, what eyes! I thought she was consoling herself with him.'

'Perhaps she'll turn up yet.'

But Dixie shook her head. 'No, she's gone, poor Kate. Gone forever.'

The cottage remained empty. The storm must have damaged one of the walls, because it toppled soon afterwards, and the building was no longer habitable. The spirit of the place, that 'take me as I am' air Kate had sensed when she first saw it, was finally broken. It was a silent spot and rather creepy, and people didn't like to go there. Sometimes a white cat was seen, peering out from the wild garden, but no-one had ever been able to catch it. As the months passed, the stones of the cottage fell or mysteriously disappeared and then reappeared in new homes about the district, or in the walls farmers erected on their land. Only the river remained the same.

As for Devlin's ghost, when the moon was full and mist danced on the water and curlews cried their mournful warning, it was said the boatman still rowed the river. But now he had a companion, a fair-haired woman who sat with him and smiled and trailed her fingers in the water. And it was only natural that woman should become known as 'Kate', and that she, too, should pass into local legend.